MONSTER vs. BOY

MONSTER vs. BOY

Karen Krossing

Charlesbridge

Text copyright © 2023 by Karen Krossing
Jacket illustrations copyright © 2023 by Markia Jenai
All rights reserved, including the right of reproduction in whole or in part in any form. Charlesbridge and colophon are registered trademarks of Charlesbridge Publishing, Inc.

At the time of publication, all URLs printed in this book were accurate and active. Charlesbridge, the author, and the illustrator are not responsible for the content or accessibility of any website.

Published by Charlesbridge
9 Galen Street, Watertown, MA 02472
(617) 926-0329 • www.charlesbridge.com

Library of Congress Cataloging-in-Publication Data
Names: Krossing, Karen, 1965– author.
Title: Monster vs. boy / Karen Krossing.
Other titles: Monster versus boy
Description: Watertown, MA: Charlesbridge, 2023. | Audience: Ages 10–12. | Audience: Grades 4–6. | Summary: As eleven-year-old Dawz and Mim, the terrifying but kind-hearted monster who lives in his closet, become more aware of each other, they must uncover the true nature of their mysterious connection.
Identifiers: LCCN 2022012914 (print) | LCCN 2022012915 (ebook) | ISBN 9781623543563 (hardcover) | ISBN 9781632893284 (ebook)
Subjects: LCSH: Monsters—Juvenile fiction. | Magic—Juvenile fiction. | Interpersonal relations—Juvenile fiction. | Books and reading—Juvenile fiction. | Fear—Juvenile fiction. | CYAC: Monsters—Fiction. | Magic—Fiction. | Interpersonal relations—Fiction. | Books and reading—Fiction. | Fear—Fiction. | Fantasy. | LCGFT: Monster fiction. | Fantasy fiction.
Classification: LCC PZ7.K9355 Mo 2023 (print) | LCC PZ7.K9355 (ebook) | DDC 813.6 [Fic]—dc23/eng/20220426
LC record available at https://lccn.loc.gov/2022012914
LC ebook record available at https://lccn.loc.gov/2022012915

Printed in the United States of America
(hc) 10 9 8 7 6 5 4 3 2 1

Illustration done digitally using Clip Studio Paint
Display type set in Colby Condensed Medium Italic by Jason Vandenberg
Text type set in New Century Schoolbook © Adobe Systems Incorporated
Printed by Maple Press in York, Pennsylvania, USA
Production supervision by Mira Kennedy
Designed by Cathleen Schaad

For you,
and your
monster too.

Chapter 1

In the way-up north, the town of Morsh squatted on a rocky mound surrounded by a forest. It was north of the bustle of the big city. West of cottage country with its crowded lakes and roaring motorboats. And southeast of a mucky marsh that liked to lead hikers in circles before releasing them tired and confused. Morsh was a town where black bears didn't live in pens, and most people believed that dangerous and magical creatures had once haunted the place. As if the land used to breed monsters but had forgotten how.

The shops in Morsh sold hiking gear and maps of long-ago monster sightings to delighted tourists. At Four Corners—the crossroads at the center of town—a statue of a giant bearlike beast towered on its hind legs, mouth open in a silent roar and claws raised. Tourists posed for photos with it. Townsfolk decorated it during holidays.

In this town lived a boy who kept his distance from the Bear Beast statue, which looked like it might break free and chase him down Main Street. The boy's mom had named him Dawson, but when his little sister, Jayla, learned to talk, she shortened it to Dawz.

Jayla and Dawz. Dawz and Jayla.

Dawz didn't like to think about Mom or the small apartment in the big city where they'd once lived. He didn't like to think about how weird Mom had become before she left—mumbling to herself about yellow feathers and a scorpion tail, and forgetting to make dinner night after night. Now Dawz and Jayla lived with Pop in a ramshackle house on the outskirts of town, where Pop's kitchen was always busy and bubbling.

Pop was really their uncle, although he'd adopted them on a warm summer day years ago. That day, they'd toasted with fizzy apple drinks and shared a peach cobbler Dawz helped to make. Pop had let him slice the peaches, mix the batter for the topping, and sprinkle the sugary-cinnamon mix over it all. Jayla had poured the drinks with only one spill.

The three of them were a mismatched crew—Pop skinny as a celery stalk with long ash-brown hair and pale skin, Jayla shaped like a pumpkin with pecan-brown pom-pom ponytails and bronze skin, and Dawz in the middle with wavy brown bangs that fell in his eyes and sourdough skin. Dawz wished they looked more like one another, but they were a family in all the ways that mattered.

No one in their ramshackle house knew that a monster—who was smaller than a bear cub—lived in Dawz's bedroom closet on the third floor. But Dawz suspected. A niggling prickle at the edge of his left eye told him so.

Chapter 2

The monster lived in the boy's closet. She called herself Mim. No one had ever spoken her name. Not the boy. Not the grown-up who tucked blankets over the boy each night. Mim was a name for herself. Her own delightful secret.

Still, she wouldn't mind sharing her secret with someone else.

The boy's closet was nestled against the roof of the house. Or was it Mim's closet? She couldn't remember. She'd been there such a long time. And time had a way of scrambling her memories with her daydreams.

Mim couldn't remember before the closet, or if she'd ever been outside it. She couldn't remember how she got there, or when it happened. She just knew that the closet was her safe place in a world that felt too big to explore.

This closet—she decided it must be hers—had odd nooks that poked into the eaves before they spilled into the wide space by the door. Mim knew all the nooks. The narrow one. The high-up one.

She also knew what was in every box, bag, and barrel. Yes, there was a barrel. A blue plastic one filled with a tent without poles, a dragon costume, and holey sweaters—the scratchy kind. Mim had crawled into every container. She'd shaped a nest out of ribbons and wrap. She'd built a tower of books that teetered and fell. Then she'd built it again and again. She liked how the crashing noise rumbled through the floorboards. How it made the boy call out in his sleep. How it made him grip his blanket under his chin and watch the crack in the closet door with his eyes wide as moons.

Yes. Mim growled her best monster growl, releasing a puff of smoke and ash from her nostrils. *I like my boy this way.*

Mim watched the boy through that same crack and sometimes the keyhole in her door. They lined up with his bed, and only his bed.

He was no trouble when he was sleeping. Then, he breathed peaceful sounds—*shoosh-swip, shoosh-swip.* She liked the rhythm of it.

But when he got as wild as the wind against the roof—waving a glowing stick, yelling "Take that, you villain," and chasing a larger boy over and around the bed—then Mim hid in her nest of ribbons and wrap with her hands around her knees and her hooves tucked under her.

No. Mim flattened her stub tail against her. *I do not like my boy that way.*

5

Mim watched the boy cough and sneeze in his bed. She watched him cry once, but she didn't know why he was upset. She watched until he moved out of her view. Where did he go?

He disappeared on most days. While he was gone, she sprawled across a box of wooden blocks until they left marks on her scales.

But most evenings, he came into her view. The grown-up came too, and the small girl—long enough to share a book. Mim knew the word *grown-up* meant "big person." She'd learned words like that because of books.

Mim had discovered that books could be used for more than building towers and crashing. She'd watched the boy, grown-up, and girl burrow under blankets with a book. The boy usually rested his head on the grown-up's shoulder, and the girl did too, their faces aglow in a circle of lamplight. Mim didn't want to burrow with them, and she didn't like the too-bright light, but their circle also filled up with words. The grown-up held the book as he spoke them, and Mim suspected they came out of the book.

Those words slithered and leaped within that small circle. They made the boy's limbs grow still. They set his eyes ablaze. They brought a smile to his face like a playful shadow.

Mim could only guess at how those books fired him up and tamed him all at once. But they did.

Books were powerful. Wonders dwelled inside them. Wonders that Mim was missing, alone in her dusty closet.

Luckily, the grown-up's words spilled beyond the circle of light too. They flipped and flapped across the room. They danced and wriggled through the crack and the keyhole in her closet door. They visited Mim in the most tail-flapping ways.

They built stories that lived inside her and kept her company. They formed creatures that felt realer than real, like friends come to play. She adored the gigantic wolf-humans of most fearsome terribleness. She cheered for the lake serpents with barbed fins. One of her favorites were the jumbies who watched children from the forest. They made Mim's purple scales shiver and her gray fur rustle. Jumbies spied from the shadows, like Mim did.

Books were magical.

Although the endings of stories haunted Mim. The story-children defeated the wolf-humans. They hunted the lake serpents. They chased the jumbies. Over and over, Mim had to plug her ears when the stories ended.

If only a book could end in a better way.

Yet what haunted Mim more than story endings was a question. How did a book beam words into the grown-up's mouth? If only Mim could control the words from a book. Then she'd be powerful enough to tame the boy. Magical enough to create story friends. Friends that could never be defeated.

But when Mim opened one of her books, nothing happened.

Maybe she couldn't make a book work by herself. After all, the grown-up had the boy and the girl to help.

Maybe she needed someone else to help her unlock the magic.

She found a rather large spider in the high-up nook where the wind whistled in. First, she nestled next to the spider, as the boy did with his grown-up. One of her horns poked near the spider's web, which was a kind of nest, so Mim was careful not to knock it loose. Next, she opened the book. It was full of squiggly black marks arranged in rows, like ants marching in lines through her closet. The marks were as thin as the spider's legs, and they bent into strange shapes. Some shapes stood straight and tall. Others circled and curved. Many shapes repeated. None of them moved or spoke to her. Neither did the spider.

She turned the pages just like the grown-up had. She opened her mouth, anticipating a spill of words over her lips. Would they tickle? She hoped they wouldn't hurt.

Nothing.

Mim shook the book at the spider. "Why aren't you making it work?"

More nothing.

A moth fluttered into view . . . and into the spider's web. Could the moth help? Mim held the book so they could all see. She opened her mouth wider than wide. *Please come*, she begged the words.

The spider hurried to the moth and began to wrap it in its silk.

How upsetting for the moth. How lucky for the spider.

Mim turned away. Maybe the spider wasn't the right someone. Same for the moth.

Maybe she needed a particular someone to make the book work. Maybe that someone was the boy.

Mim had seen the boy open books and turn pages when he was by himself, but words didn't come out of his mouth then. He *had* made a book work when the girl nestled with him. Then he'd spoken words that made the girl laugh and Mim prickle because she didn't want to hear the boy speak a book at her. She wanted books to beam words into *her* mouth.

But the boy was not a helpful someone. He would never show Mim how to make a book work. Mim knew that like she knew her own name.

She would have to force him.

But how?

Mim pressed herself into the high-up nook. She breathed in the mysterious scents that traveled on the breeze. One day, fresh and damp. Another day, sooty and sour. Scents that promised delights but troubles too. And she pondered how to make the boy unlock the magic of a book.

Could she capture him when he entered the closet, even though the boy rarely came near anymore?

Could she rush out at him while he slept, even though she'd have to open her closet door and step out into the world?

A world that smelled shivery delicious.

A world that might be too wide to see at once.

A world that felt too vast for a small closet monster who had named herself Mim.

Chapter 3

Outside the closet, in his attic room, the boy named Dawz bounced high on his mini-trampoline but not high enough to hit the ceiling.

He gazed out his three windows that faced different directions, so he could see anything coming at him from street, forest, or marsh.

He traced the monstrous constellations on his blanket—like the hydra that Hercules defeated—and read about them in books.

And he locked his bedroom door to keep Jayla out after he'd pranked her—maybe by leaving whipped cream in her slippers.

Dawz's room fit him just right. Except for his closet.

It was almost as big as his whole room. It had a crawl space into the eaves and odd crevices like the cavities in the old, yellow teeth his dentist had once shown him to convince him to floss more. It was crammed with a jumble of junk no one used.

"It smells worse than wet dog," Dawz told his friend Atlas. "Worse than campfire smoke."

At night, when Dawz woke from a bad dream, he often heard strange sounds coming from his closet. Footsteps. *Shuffle, shuffle* sounds. Then—*crash!*

Dawz kept his clothes in his dresser drawers.

He knew that most eleven-year-olds weren't afraid of a closet. Atlas wasn't, but he had shoulders that were wide enough to scare off most things. That was why Dawz had nicknamed him Atlas—after the Greek Titan who held up the sky on his shoulders. Also, Atlas was part Greek, which made the nickname even better. Dawz sometimes wished he and Atlas were brothers. Dawz's own family was townsfolk from way back.

Luiza, a retired town councilor who told the best stories, said foolish settlers from across the sea were the first to inhabit this place—a place where no Indigenous people wanted to set foot. Perhaps because of the strange growls and yips that echoed through the forest and marsh. Perhaps monsters really had roamed back then. If Luiza's story was true, the settlers got lost in the marsh, camped on the first dry ground they could find, and never left. They called the town Morsh—a mashup of *monstrous marsh*—and the name stuck. The town of Morsh by the Monstrous Marsh. Good for tourists who loved scary tales. Not good for a boy who worried they might be true.

On the day Atlas opened Dawz's closet just to explore the jumble of junk, he pulled out a sponge and a pair of broken flippers.

"Let's play flipper badminton." Atlas lobbed the sponge above his head, then smacked it toward Dawz with a flipper.

"Wait!" Dawz tried to close the closet door first, but the sponge came at him fast. Then he had trouble hitting it back because he worried the whole time the closet door was open, as if *something* might escape.

It was a silly worry. Only little kids were afraid of closets. Except for his sister, who wasn't afraid of much, even though she was three years younger.

Dawz wished he could be as fearless as Jayla.

After the flipper badminton game, Dawz kept his closet door locked all the time. The lock was old-fashioned with a keyhole he could see through and a tarnished brass key that wobbled in the lock. Since it didn't seem secure, he also began to set traps outside the closet door each night, except when Atlas slept over. Sometimes, he'd sprinkle Froot Loops on the floor around the closet door so if anything tried to escape, he'd wake to crunching footsteps. Other times, he'd stack some books so they'd tumble over if the door opened. But he always tidied up his traps in the morning before Pop or Jayla saw them. He didn't want them to know he was worried about weird stuff like closet monsters. It reminded him of Mom and her strange talk about yellow feathers and a scorpion tail, and Dawz wanted to be normal, like Pop.

As he got older, Dawz spent more time in Pop's kitchen. Pop was a freelance chef, and he had two ovens, spoons in all sizes, and silver pots Dawz could see his face in. One of Dawz's best kitchen memories was when Pop taught him and Atlas about the magic of baker's yeast.

"Mix salt, sugar, flour, and oil together, and what do you get? Flat bread." Pop wiped his floury hands on his apron. "But add yeast—ah! That's when the magic happens."

Dawz and Atlas learned to dissolve yeast in warm water. To mix it with other ingredients. To knead dough, let it rise, punch it down, let it rise again. The sweet, sharp smell of yeast! The air bubbles it magicked into the dough! The scent of baking bread. The warm buttery taste. Pop was a wizard in the kitchen, and Dawz wanted to be one too.

So, on a rainy Saturday when Pop promised Dawz and Atlas the use of any ingredients in the kitchen if they kept Jayla busy for the morning, they played hide-and-seek with her, even though they were too old for it.

Of course, Dawz didn't want to hide in his closet. He didn't want to go anywhere near it.

But then Jayla was "it" for the second time, and he could hear her footsteps on the creaky stairs to his attic. He'd already hidden in his laundry basket, and under the bed was too obvious.

He hurried over to his closet door with the key, unlocked it, and put his hand on the knob. Already, he was sweating.

"I hear you in there," Jayla called from the stairs. "Is that you, Dawz?"

He forced his fingers to turn the knob. He couldn't let his sister find him first—again—just because he was afraid of a closet. He yanked open the door and stepped inside, shutting it behind him. He stumbled over a tumble of books, dove behind a blue barrel, and crouched there, listening.

Who's afraid of a closet? He glared into the shadows to scare off anything that might be lurking.

Chapter 4

When the boy opened her closet door, Mim picked up the nearest book. She didn't mean to. Her hands did it all by themselves.

He's not a helpful someone, she reminded herself. Mim held the book against her chest—partly as a shield, like warriors did in the stories she'd heard the grown-up speak; partly as a weapon if the boy got too close; and partly because she was determined to force him to make the words come out of it, one way or another.

How nice it would be to make a book work.

This might be her only chance.

The boy peered around as if he couldn't see in the dark closet.

Good. Let him stumble and fall. Then she'd pounce on him and shove the book in his face.

He shut her closet door with a *click*. He crept behind her blue barrel and crouched there, still but alert.

Maybe she should wait until he was off guard.

But Mim's feet moved against her will—as if she was losing control of her body one part at a time. Her feet stepped out from the narrow nook, which was the deepest one. They dodged a box of trophies and a bunch of dusty aprons hanging from a hook.

When her feet stopped, Mim peeked from behind a tower of books she'd built, ready for crashing.

The boy was close enough to make her scales crawl. Close enough to see his beady eyes and rash of freckles.

"Come out, come out, wherever you are," a voice called from beyond her closet door.

Mim cowered. The voice was the small girl's, but her words were strange. Why would Mim come out of her safe closet, especially when she had the boy where she wanted him? The boy hunched lower, so he didn't seem interested in leaving Mim's closet either. And he still hadn't noticed her.

She should attack now. But would the girl interfere?

Mim's stub tail twitched. She couldn't lose this chance.

She popped her head—furry snout, horns, and all—out from behind the books.

He didn't move.

She tiptoed closer. One hand gripped the book. She raised her other hand, fingernails ready to claw if he tried to hurt her. Mim's snout quivered. It made her teeth rattle.

The boy looked her way. His eyes bulged. She clutched the book tighter, ready to hide behind it.

Such fear in his eyes! She snarled, puffing out smoke and ash. She liked him scared. It was better than scary.

Tackle him now, she thought. *Force him to reveal how a book works.* But her feet refused to get closer. Was she a real monster if she was too scared to tackle a boy?

A mask of hard crossed his face as if he was turning to stone before her eyes. It reminded Mim of the story monster she had heard the grown-up mention, the one who had snakes for hair and could turn her enemies to stone. Might Mim have that power?

But no, the boy shifted, then moved his arm. Mim wasn't that lucky.

Then he picked up a book. A book!

Mim dared to hope.

The boy let out a piercing scream and threw the book at her head.

Mim dove behind a stack of boxes, tail trembling.

The book landed near her with its pages bent. She wanted to straighten them, but another book came at her, then another sailed over the boxes to hit her on her snout.

Foolish! She'd been foolish. She should have attacked sooner. She should have attacked when he was sleeping.

Her precious books thunked. A pot lid clanged. Sweaters fell short of where she hid. Mim disappeared into the deepest deep of the narrowest nook. She huddled with a book between her two curved horns like a helmet.

Please don't find me, she pleaded over and over.

The boy wasn't safe. He was horrible. He was careless with books.

She would never let him in her closet again.

The horrible boy threw and threw until Mim's closet door opened, and light flooded everywhere.

Mim's eyes burned as the light beamed. *What now?*

The girl stood in the doorway, a round silhouette with two balls of hair on either side of her head. She tugged the cord to turn on the light. Then she yelled, "I see you, Dawz! You're it!"

What does that mean? Mim squinted into the light, hoping this girl wouldn't attack too. What a mistake Mim had made—letting herself be seen. She wouldn't do it again.

The girl swatted the horrible boy on his shoulder—just as the grown-up appeared in the doorway too.

"What happened? Who's hurt?" He wore an apron and gripped a large spoon.

"I won hide-and-seek *again*," the girl said, "and he made a mess." She pointed to Mim's closet floor.

Mim surveyed the damage. It wasn't just a mess. Her cozy nest was overturned. Her books hurt. The horrible boy was pure destruction.

"But I heard screaming," the grown-up said, "like someone had—"

A laugh burst out of the horrible boy with the force of a sneeze, startling Mim. He clamped a hand over his mouth, but a strangled sound escaped. "We're fine," he sputtered. "I was just trying to scare Jayla."

The grown-up shook his head like he was banishing a terrible thought.

The horrible boy scrambled out of Mim's closet.

Yes, go, she urged.

If he ever helped her unlock a book, it would surely feel like barbs and thorns, not a cozy circle of words. She needed another way.

"I'm not scared," the girl said.

"I'm glad everyone's okay." The grown-up's gaze landed on the mess. "I've been meaning to clean this closet for years."

"I like it messy." The horrible boy slammed Mim's closet door shut, but she could still hear his voice through it. "Yup, nothing like a mess."

Mim seethed. She would make a mess of his room. How would he like that? That is, if she found the courage to step outside her closet.

"That's more than a mess," said the grown-up. "We really should clean it."

"I'm hungry," the horrible boy said. "Let's make lunch now."

"You only want lunch because you're it," the girl said.

"I want lunch because Atlas and I are going to make Waffles of Extreme Greatness."

"Oooh, can they have marshmallows?"

Mim heard them moving away. Finally.

"Maybe. We need to invent a new recipe for the Bakers' Brawl." The horrible boy's voice grew fainter. "Come on. Let's find Atlas first."

"Okay, but I really like marshmallows. I'm sure the Bakers' Brawl judges will too."

Mim strained, but she could only hear footsteps fading into silence. Gorgeous silence.

She didn't move yet though. She had to be sure.

The horrible boy could be tricky.

She waited and waited. She curled into a ball for comfort. She made plans for giant towers of books that would block her closet doorway and traps that would keep the horrible boy out. And she wondered how she could unlock the magic of a book without him.

Maybe a book needed a pleasant someone to work. A friend. The horrible boy certainly wasn't a friend. But someone else could be.

Chapter 5

Dawz was usually good at making Waffles of Extreme Greatness. He usually prepped the batter, which was a basic combo of flour, sugar, and salt with oil, eggs, and milk. Atlas usually gathered other ingredients they might use. Together, they'd decide how to give their waffles Extreme Greatness by adding unusual ingredients. Smoked black forest ham and feta cheese. Or wild blueberries with spicy jalapenos. The Bakers' Brawl judges preferred strange and delicious combos, but not too strange.

The Bakers' Brawl was a local bake-off, where the judges created a new challenge each year, like who could make Cupcakes of Extreme Greatness. Contestants could combine any ingredients, but they needed to taste awesome together.

Yet today, Dawz didn't feel like he could create anything awesome. Even when he and Atlas put on their matching chef's hats and did their special handshake, Dawz felt wrong from the inside out.

Their chef's hats had been a present from Pop on the day they decided to enter their first Bakers' Brawl contest in the junior division. They weren't the traditional white hats with mushroom tops, but cool flat black beanies that tied at the back. "If you're going to follow in my footsteps"—Pop had beamed—"you need to look the part." Pop had won the contest so many times that he'd become a judge in the adult division. Dawz and Atlas had entered twice, but they'd never beaten those twin girls from Sudbury who'd won twice.

Most days, Dawz worried he'd never be as good a baker as Pop. Today, he dropped eggshells in the bowl instead of the compost bin. Today, he slopped the batter on the counter when he mixed it with his super-fast stirring method. Today, he'd seen a monster in his closet. Really seen it.

But no one else had. No. One. Else.

He'd always suspected some vile thing lived in there. The prickle at the edge of his left eye had warned him. Now, if he told the others, he would sound like Mom, muttering about yellow feathers and a scorpion tail like she'd seen a monster too. Had she?

He remembered then how she used to watch the sky from their apartment balcony, her eyes scanning nearby rooftops as she picked at the skin around her fingernails. It made him watch the sky too and worry about why it needed to be watched. Once, a flock of geese flew overhead, and she shrieked and darted inside. When he called in to say he'd watch the sky for her, she yelled at him to stop.

Dawz stirred the batter extra hard. He couldn't be like her. He couldn't have a monster living in his closet. And now, Pop wanted to clean it?

Dawz would rather lock it with a million keys and barricade it with a billion chains.

A sweet-smelling haze streamed from one of Pop's ovens, gathered above their heads, and refused to leave. Pop hurried to open the oven door. Dawz waved the haze away. Jayla ignored it. Atlas slid a window up, letting rainy gusts of spring carry it out and away.

"Thanks, Atlas," Dawz said, and Atlas grunted back. He had a full range of grunts and gestures that Dawz had learned to decode. This grunt was midrange combined with a head nod, meaning, *I got you, bro.*

Pop whirled between the oven and a mixing bowl of icing, his hair tucked under a Bakers' Brawl cap. On one long counter sat rows of cookies and cupcakes—half-iced. Jayla set four places opposite Dawz on the island counter. Atlas plopped a bag of mini-marshmallows next to Dawz, along with a boiled lobster claw, refried beans, potatoes, maple syrup, mayo, cucumbers, avocado, and blackberry jam.

"Marshmallows, marshmallows, marshmallows," Jayla chanted. She climbed onto a stool and rapped her knife and fork on the counter.

Atlas smiled at Jayla, then lifted the lobster claw toward Dawz as if to say, *What goes with marshmallows?*

Dawz tried to remember if the monster had claws, but he hadn't been able to tell in the dark. "Lobster could work," he said, trying not to second-guess himself. "Salty and sweet would be tasty."

"Good thinking," Pop said from across the room.

"But not these." Atlas put the can of refried beans back in the cupboard.

"Yeah, too weird," said Dawz. Like a boy who could see a monster.

As Atlas and Dawz considered each ingredient, Dawz tried to feel better. After all, he liked making up recipes, and he liked Atlas. They'd met shortly after Dawz and Jayla had moved in with Pop, who helped to supply Thea's Café—the allergy-friendly shop that one of Atlas's moms owned and ran by herself. Atlas's other mom, Mandi, was away on a peacekeeping mission in a faraway country because she worked in the armed forces as a real-life hero. Dawz knew Atlas was happier when both parents were home, although he was lucky enough to be able to see Mandi when she was on leave.

Dawz didn't even know his own dad's name, or Jayla's dad's either. But they had Pop, and that counted for something.

Eventually, Dawz and Atlas settled on avocado and marshmallow with a blackberry drizzle. Pop pulled out another batch of his cookies and finished icing his cupcakes. Jayla cheered when Atlas lifted the first Waffle of Extreme Greatness off the iron. After Dawz added the drizzle, it was a crispy green-and-purple glory that made everyone's mouths water. But that wasn't the best part. Dawz loved watching people eat the food they'd created.

"Yum," Jayla said with her mouth full. She shut her eyes while she chewed, and her face got a dreamy look.

"You kids inspire me." Pop held his plate out for seconds. "You're not afraid to take risks."

Dawz let out a long breath. Risks in the kitchen were worth it when Pop liked their new recipe. He didn't ask for seconds often, which meant this combo really was good. Dawz hated the frozen waffles Mom used to serve. She always toasted them wrong—burnt on the outside and still cold inside. He vowed never to eat her waffles again, even if Mom showed up without warning and forced them on him.

"We're gonna win the Bakers' Brawl this year for sure," Atlas said. The contest was only a week away, and they'd been practicing new and old recipes for ages, trying to guess what the challenge might be this year. Would it be Waffles of Extreme Greatness?

"We have to win." Suddenly, Dawz wanted that trophy more than ever. He wanted to see Pop's grin as he and Atlas held it high. To prove he was a kitchen wizard too, that he'd earned his place in Pop's kitchen—not just as an adopted son but as a real one.

Dawz and Atlas did their special handshake again, which started with a fist bump and ended with jazz hands. Then Atlas hummed the Bakers' Brawl theme song. Soon, they were both marching around the island while belting out the lyrics:

> "Pizza, pretzels, pie, or cake.
> What will you make for the Bakers' Brawl?
> Chop and knead, stir and toast.
> Who'll win it all at the Bakers' Brawl?"

"Can I enter too? Please, Pop?" Jayla said, and Dawz stopped singing. He wanted Pop to say no. Jayla didn't even like baking. It was his thing. He shouldn't have to share it with her. Besides, she didn't even have a partner, and every junior contestant had to bake with a partner.

"Next year you'll be old enough," Pop told her.

"But a year's so far away." Jayla pouted for a moment before she said, "Maybe I'll be a wrestler instead. Are there wrestling contests for kids?"

"We can find you one," Dawz said. Wrestling suited Jayla like baking suited him.

"Of course we can," Pop said. "Now, let's clean up here, then get to work on that closet."

As Dawz took off his chef's hat, all the wrong feelings flooded back.

"Can we do it later?" He thought up an excuse. "Atlas and I were going to ride our bikes." He hated lying to Pop. It was like sharing a recipe without listing all the ingredients. The dish would never work out, and Pop would never know why. It was a huge betrayal since Pop had always shared his recipes with Dawz, even the secret ones he kept from customers, and Dawz had tried to be honest about most things too. But admit he'd seen a monster in his closet? Dawz didn't know how to have that conversation, especially with Pop. He just knew that he had to keep that closet door locked with the monster inside, no matter what. He felt like a guardian of the gate, which sounded like a story he'd like to read, not live through.

Atlas gave him a quizzical look. *Biking in the rain?*

"Think of it as a treasure hunt," Pop said. "Who knows what we'll find in there?"

Chapter 6

The silence lingered inside Mim's closet and outside too. It wrapped around her like a blanket. Gradually, her hearts slowed—both of them. She stood and stretched, hoping she was safe now.

Just to be sure, Mim listened at her closet door . . . and heard voices. One, two, three, four! So many voices at once!

She scampered for the narrow nook, tripping over boxes. She heard her closet door yank open. Light speared the shadows as she crouched in the nook, panting. Who was coming? Would they hurt her? Would they be a friend?

"This old closet gives me the creeps." The grown-up waded into the books, reckless and uncaring. "Maybe that's why I never clean it."

"I think it's cool. We could make a fort in here." The girl bounded ahead of the grown-up, and Mim tucked into herself with her hands over her snout.

"Tree forts are more fun," the horrible boy said. "We should definitely build one of those instead. Let's start now."

His voice sent a shudder through Mim. She'd promised herself she'd never let him in again, yet here he was.

"I like tree forts," the larger boy said. He didn't fill up her closet with lots of talk, but the width of him scared her. He filled up her doorway.

"Well, let's get to it." The grown-up gathered up the tent. "Toss out anything broken. We'll donate what we don't use anymore."

A spark flared inside Mim's chest, where it pinged from heart to heart, faster and faster. This was *her* closet. How dare they touch anything!

Mim wanted a friend to help her make a book work but not like this. Not with any of *them*.

Then the invaders were moving Mim's boxes. So many scents at once. So many footsteps stomping across her overturned nest of ribbons and wrap. Except for the horrible boy, who lurked at the entrance to her closet, peering around.

"Be careful," he called to the girl as she climbed over the pile of books he'd thrown.

The grown-up passed him some of Mim's thickest books—the best ones for building towers. "For the donation pile," he said. "I haven't read these cookbooks in years, but someone else will want them."

Mim didn't know what a donation pile was. She just knew that the horrible boy was stacking *her* things outside her closet.

Then the larger boy plunged into Mim's narrow nook. She held her breath, fairly certain he was too wide to fit all the way in.

"Don't!" the horrible boy shrieked. "Anything could be back there!" He lunged into Mim's closet, pushing through the mess and past the grown-up and the girl.

"You mean like Bakers' Brawl trophies?" The larger boy's voice boomed in her ears. "Wow, so many! Cool aprons too. This one has a polar bear with wings on it." The larger boy was eating, his hand reaching into his pocket every now and then to retrieve a snack and pop it in his mouth. *Chomp, chomp, chomp* went his jaws.

Mim shivered, imagining his teeth chomping down on her. She readied her fingernails. They weren't pointed, but they were thick enough to gouge his skin if she had to scare him away.

"My trophies!" the grown-up said. "I forgot they were here."

The spark inside Mim flared—they were hers! She used them when an itch sneaked between her scales and wouldn't budge.

As the grown-up picked up her box and carried it out, her trophies clattered together. "Here's my first trophy ever," he said from outside her closet.

How could she get her things back?

"You know, I didn't win my first few contests either. But I got better with practice, just like you boys. I have a good feeling about you two this year."

"So do I," the larger boy called out. "Who was your partner when you were in junior division?"

"That would be Faye—my sister." The grown-up reentered Mim's closet and picked up another one of her boxes. How could she stop him?

"Dawz told me Mom was a terrible cook," the girl said. "Was that why you lost?"

"Of course not! Faye had unusual ideas that didn't always work. But when they did, they were spectacular. She made those aprons for us. New ones for every contest we entered."

"You never told me she could sew." The girl turned to the horrible boy.

"I didn't know." The horrible boy scowled. "Do we have to talk about her?"

"But you never want to talk about her."

"Pop says I don't have to, if I don't want to."

"Hey, could I borrow an apron for the Junior Bakers' Brawl?" The larger boy turned to her boy. "We could each wear one."

The horrible boy moved close enough for his scent to overpower Mim. Sweet with a nasty tang.

"Why? They're old. And I bet they smell. Everything in here does." He glanced around, probably searching for her.

The larger boy sniffed one of Mim's aprons. "Smells fine to me. And they're so cool! We'd look awesome."

"I don't know. I'd feel . . . weird." A strange look crossed the horrible boy's face, and he focused straight at Mim as if he knew she'd be hiding there.

Mim's scales rippled. How had he known where to find her? Could he sense her?

She hissed, loud enough to scare both boys.

Terror crept over the horrible boy's face like an army of spiders, but the larger boy was too stupid to notice.

"Did you hear that?" the horrible one whispered to his friend. He pointed right at Mim.

She hissed again.

"Did I hear what?" The larger boy peered. "What are you pointing at?"

"What do you mean? Can't you see the monster? At the back of that nook?"

"Quit kidding." The larger boy turned back to the aprons. "Which one do you like?"

"But it's right there!" The horrible boy's voice cracked, and something cracked inside Mim too. She had to be visible to more than the horrible boy!

"What are you looking at?" The girl was suddenly at the horrible boy's elbow, and he jumped. Behind them, the grown-up was heaving the blue barrel out of Mim's closet.

"Nothing." The horrible boy stepped between Mim and the girl like he was protecting her. "I . . . I must be seeing shadows. And hearing the wind."

Mim was more than a shadow. More than wind. She hissed louder than loud to scare off the girl, the larger boy—everyone.

The girl gazed toward Mim, unseeing.

No, no, no! It couldn't be. How could she be a good monster if she could only scare one horrible boy?

Mim stood. She raked the air with her fingernails.

The horrible boy flinched.

The girl turned away. "What's under here?" She lifted Mim's overturned nest.

"Looks like wrapping paper," the larger boy said. "And lots of ribbons."

The girl poked at Mim's nest, but Mim couldn't take her eyes off the horrible boy, whose eyes drilled back into hers. Were they connected? She didn't want to share anything with him. Not her closet. Not her boxes and books. Not the air they both breathed.

The horrible boy broke eye contact first.

"Let's just get everything out of here," he said. "We can sort it in my room." He shoved one box away from her nook and another, clearing a space around her hiding spot.

Mim puffed out a cloud of smoke and ash as big as her hand.

"Good idea," the grown-up said. "Why don't you pass out those boxes at the back?"

Soon, they were all shoving and carrying everything out of her closet, leaving Mim with an empty, echoing space.

She clawed and puffed, but no one reacted except the horrible boy. He never turned his back on her, but he never warned the others either.

Like she was not a threat.

Like she was just a shadow.

Chapter 7

By the time Pop and Jayla disappeared downstairs with the last of the boxes to donate or toss out, Dawz's insides were bubbling like a pot of Pop's pasta. He felt hot. Twitchy. He couldn't sit still or rest, even though he was tired from moving boxes. The way the monster had clawed. Puffed smoke. Threatened his people. Dawz locked the closet door and got busy stacking books in front of it.

"What are you doing?" Atlas asked.

Dawz's insides boiled hotter. If he explained, Atlas might think he was weird or something worse. But it would be easier than talking to Pop, and Dawz could use some help with keeping the monster in. Right now, it would be plotting ways to hurt him.

Dawz took a chance. He told Atlas why he needed to barricade the door. He described the monster and how it had hissed but only he noticed. And he kept busy stacking books in front of the door. He wanted it barricaded as soon as possible, but he also didn't want to watch Atlas. If he looked freaked out, Dawz didn't want to see it.

"And you really couldn't see it?" Dawz asked as he shoved his last stack of books into place. His barricade didn't look like enough to stop a monster.

Dawz risked a glance at Atlas, who stood in the middle of the room like an immovable island. As Dawz watched, he shook his head, gazing at the locked closet door with shock and awe.

"Wow, a real monster! I've hoped for this, but . . . what should we do with it?" he asked.

Dawz sucked in a breath, relieved that his friend believed him, that he hadn't judged him or laughed at him. "Nothing. We shouldn't go anywhere near it." He tried to shove his whole bookcase in front of the barricade, but it didn't budge.

"Should we tell your pop?"

"No!" Pop would probably think Dawz was making up stories. Or worse—he'd think Dawz was . . . different. Pop was too sensible—too down-to-earth—to ever be able to see a monster. He never wanted to read bedtime stories about monsters, but he did because Dawz and Jayla asked for them. He didn't like to listen to Luiza's stories about the monsters that used to haunt the town either. Pop liked to read cookbooks and guidebooks about which wild plants they could eat.

Atlas crossed his arms and grunted low, meaning he didn't agree but would go along with it. Together, they pushed the bookshelf into place, then stepped back to stare at the barricade and what lay beyond it.

"It's really in there?" Atlas asked.

"I saw it and smelled it too. It was breathing out clouds of smoke. . . ." Dawz shook off the memory. It made it more real in his mind. He could see the monster when he shut his eyes, as if it was right in front of him instead of behind a locked and barricaded closet door.

Atlas grabbed one of Dawz's cryptozoology books off the barricade. "Maybe we can find it in here. Then I could see what it's like."

Dawz nodded, grateful for any ideas that would help. "Maybe we could learn its weaknesses."

Atlas and Dawz had both read a ton of books about cryptozoology—the study of creatures who are rumored but not yet proven to exist. They'd listened to the stories Luiza told wide-eyed tourists from her favorite bench near the Bear Beast statue or her favorite table in Thea's Café. It had been scary fun to try to connect her story monsters with ones from their books, even though they hadn't found any matches. But now they had a real monster to research.

Dawz had always worried that might happen.

He sat on his mini-trampoline, bouncing slightly. He flipped through his field guide of cryptid creatures as Atlas watched over his shoulder. The Thetis Lake monster, yeti, and kraken. It listed monsters who were confirmed hoaxes as well as ones who'd been proven to be real, like the rare coelacanth—a deep-sea fish with spiny fins. Supposedly, it had vanished with the dinosaurs, but Dawz's book said it could be found in the Indian Ocean and the waters near Indonesia.

"What about that?" Atlas pointed to a chupacabra—a blood-sucking dog-thing from Puerto Rico with spikes down its back. The book said it could hop like a kangaroo.

Dawz turned the page. "It's nothing like that. Plus, this monster has horns, remember?" Impressive, curved ones that made Dawz shudder.

"Okay then, maybe a jackalope?"

A jackalope was a jackrabbit with antelope horns that turned out to be fake. "Not even close. It had hooves, not rabbit feet, and a furry head like a musk ox." Dawz wondered if the fur was as sharp as quills. He hoped he never found out.

They looked through page after page of cryptids, each one a new threat now that they'd found a real monster. How many other monsters might be loose in the world? Dawz slammed the book shut, as if it would lock them all inside. "I don't think we'll find it in here."

"We've got loads more to look through."

Dawz sighed. "I guess. But this monster has different features than anything we've read about. Hooves and hands. Fur and scales. It's like a combo of creature parts, like the monsters Luiza talks about." One of her stories was about a fang-toothed bear-monster like the town's statue. Most townsfolk laughed when she said the Bear Beast had been a real creature once, but Dawz never had.

"You know what we should do?" Atlas said. "We should record everything about it. I can stay for a sleepover, so we'll have lots of time."

Dawz hadn't thought about sleeping. How would he ever sleep again, knowing the monster was on the other side of a thin wooden door?

Maybe he could sleep at Atlas's. But he wanted to

make sure the monster stayed put. If only Atlas could sleep over every night.

"We can record how tall it is," Atlas was saying. "How big its feet are—"

"Its hooves, you mean."

"Right. Hooves. We can be real cryptozoologists. Or you can, because I can't see, hear, or smell it." Atlas strode to the barricade and leaned one ear close to the door. "Do you think I could one day? I can't be a good cryptozoologist if I can't observe it."

"Don't get too close," Dawz warned. Seeing the monster was the worst thing that had happened to him.

"I'd rather know what's coming at me." Atlas reached over the bookcase to stroke the closet door. "Funny . . . but Luiza never mentioned that only one person could see the monsters."

"I'd rather not be the only one." Dawz thought about Mom then. Her mutterings must have been about a monster she'd seen. Was it somehow her fault that he could see one?

Yellow feathers—everywhere, he'd once heard her say. She'd been sweeping the balcony, even though it had looked clean to him. Then she'd sobbed. He hated that sound—the way it tore at him. He'd often wished he knew his dad, or Jayla's. Maybe one of them could've helped Mom get better or come over to make dinner when she forgot. But whenever he'd asked Mom about them, she waved him away, saying she didn't want their dads around. When he'd asked for their names or where they lived, she gazed at Dawz as if she'd forgotten.

Dawz hugged his knees to his chest. He couldn't imagine Mom competing in a Bakers' Brawl contest or sewing aprons, like Pop had said. He'd never seen her bake or sew. But for sure she'd had unusual ideas. Dawz had never told anyone about Mom's weirdness—not even Pop. It felt like something to keep hidden. He hoped she never came back, although he'd never admit it. What kind of son didn't want to see his own mother?

"Dawz, did you hear me?" Atlas said. "We should make a plan for if it escapes."

Suddenly, Dawz was exhausted. This was his life now—not only guarding this closet and keeping secrets from Pop but battling this monster if it got out. He would never be able to rest. And he didn't know if he could do it.

"Dawz?" Atlas nudged him.

"Right," Dawz said. At least he had Atlas. Dependable Atlas. "We should make a plan."

"Great, because I have some ideas." Atlas smiled like this was a fun adventure. "And it starts with lightsabers."

Chapter 8

At dusk, Mim lay snout down in her empty closet. Empty of boxes. Empty of books to share with a friend. Empty of her nest of ribbons and wrap, of scratching places, of ways to block the horrible boy from entering.

She couldn't believe it was gone. All gone.

A spring wind whooshed into the high-up nook, but Mim ignored it. It carried mysterious scents that might be musky flowers, fumes from a car, or worms squirming in dirt. It blew them around the empty space in her closet. It blew and blew until the scents tickled Mim's snout.

Forget the empty, the smells said. *Don't you want to know us?*

Mim scrambled into the high-up nook. She needed those scents to soothe her. To tell her that she could be brave enough to leave her closet. That she could find hope outside.

She lay sideways with her tail flattened and tried to press her face into the space where the wind sneaked in. Those scents, just beyond reach. Promises of a better nest. A better home. Free from the boy.

But she couldn't get into her regular position. Her horns got caught on either side of the sloped ceiling.

She tried this way and that. She shimmied. She used force. No matter what she did, the high-up nook didn't fit Mim anymore.

Had the nook shrunk? It looked the same size.

Had her horns grown? Grown!

Mim didn't need to eat, although she'd tried it every so often, just for fun. She nibbled a lace-up shoe once. It tasted dry and rubbery. She ate a dead moth. Her insides didn't like it. But whether she ate or not, Mim never grew. She could always fit in the high-up nook next to the roof.

Until the night she couldn't.

Mim climbed down to her closet floor and hurried to measure herself. She hardly stopped to notice that the crack in the door had been blocked from the other side, and the keyhole too. *Good riddance!* She didn't want to watch the horrible boy anymore.

Mim stood with her snout against the door. Usually, the top of her head fit under the doorknob. But now, the doorknob was level with her eyes! She *was* taller.

How terrible to be taller!

Mim missed her nest more than ever. To comfort herself, she curled into a ball on the hard floor—a bigger ball than ever—and tried to remember if she'd grown before.

She couldn't.

If only her memories stretched back further.

She touched her too-big horns. She examined herself all over. Her hooves looked bulbous. The gray fur on her legs and haunches had thickened. The purple scales on her upper body had lengthened. Her arms stretched on forever, ending with wider, longer hands. Her fingernails had grown too, narrowing into sort-of claws. Even her gray furry snout felt longer. What if she never stopped growing? She might grow bigger than her closet. She might grow into a human!

Anything could happen.

Her world had cracked open, and Mim didn't know how to fix it.

Mim worried and fussed until a hopeful thought crept into her brain and made a nest. Perhaps she was growing to fit the extra space in her closet. If that was true, she could never leave her closet for the wide world. No, she didn't want to grow bigger than big! But maybe, if she filled the space in her closet, she would stop growing.

She needed her ribbons and wrap back. And her books. And her boxes, barrel, and everything inside them. Mim needed her closet to be like it used to be. Then she'd build a barricade to keep the boy out. Then she'd stop growing, or maybe even shrink back to her own size.

Yes. It had to work. It must.

Mim listened at the door to check if the boy was asleep. She'd heard a lot of thumping and scraping, but the room beyond the door was silent now. She put her hand on the doorknob. Her scales rippled. Mim had never, ever ventured beyond her closet. It would be dangerous. She'd have to face the horrible boy. If only she knew how to use a book to tame him.

Please, please be asleep, she thought.

She turned the knob. It whined.

The door didn't budge.

She pushed at it. She twisted the knob this way and that. The door still didn't move.

Mim's closet had one way in and one way out. It had no windows. No loose roof boards to squeeze between. No vents to tunnel away. Her home had become a trap.

Mim leaned her horns against the door. The horrible boy had thrown books. He'd invaded her closet. He'd destroyed her nest. Now he'd locked her door.

That boy had no limits to his horribleness.

Mim could hardly bear to nest so close to him.

Once again, she wondered about seeking a new nest. But she needed her closet and her things to become small again. She had no choice.

Mim stuck her longest fingernail in the keyhole, using the new, sharp point. She had to work fast.

She had to refill her nest before she grew more.

Mim knew about keyholes from watching the boy. She'd seen him use a key to lock the door to his room. She'd heard the girl on the other side of that door, yelling to get in. She'd seen the boy laughing.

She wiggled her nail-claw around and around in the keyhole. She didn't know what she was reaching for—

it was just what the boy did with a key. She poked anything she could touch. She twisted and turned her nail-claw. She tried not to rattle the door.

Then she heard a satisfying *click*.

Something in the lock had shifted. Mim tested the door. The knob turned and . . . the door creaked open.

But only a smidge before it thudded into something.

More noise that might wake the boy. Mim listened, hoping he was still asleep. This one time, she didn't want to scare him awake.

Silence. Then gentle snores.

She knew that sound. The larger boy was in the room. Sometimes, he slept on the floor in a tube-shaped blanket nest. When that happened, the horrible boy and the larger boy talked late into the night. Then the larger boy snored just like that.

Mim pushed at her closet door. Beyond it, the something that blocked it from opening slid along the floor. The something was heavy and hard to push out of the way. Mim shoved.

Clatter, crash, BANG!

Oh no! The something had fallen. She must have woken the boys.

Mim tried to find the spark deep inside her. The one that made her feel strong enough to face two boys. Then she pressed her whole body against the door, forcing it open and shoving the something out of the way with a too-loud scraping sound.

She couldn't see her ribbons and wrap or any boxes or barrel. But in front of her lay an empty bookcase toppled on its back. To her right was a tumble of books. Books full of story friends! Maybe jumbies and wendigos. A giant yew tree that could talk.

"Get ready!" she heard the horrible boy yell.

He stood on the bed. Her horrible, horrible boy. He waved a horrible glowing stick that made her squint.

Mim shielded her body with her nail-claws.

"Can you see it?" he said.

"Where? Tell me where to aim!" The larger boy stood near Mim's closet in his blanket nest, holding another glowing stick and gazing above her head as if he still couldn't see her.

Mim shoved her closet door all the way open to prove she wasn't a shadow. The larger boy gasped in a satisfying way.

"It's in the doorway," the horrible boy shouted. "We need to force it back!"

Mim slid sideways toward the pile of books, hoping to scoop up an armful to take back to her closet. She ducked around the larger boy easily, keeping her horns aimed at the horrible one. The larger boy had his back to her now, stupidly swinging his glowing stick in the wrong direction, and for a moment, Mim was grateful to be invisible to him.

As she neared the books, the horrible boy jumped toward her, waving the glowing stick so it hurt her eyes. *Foul thing!*

She faced him across the pile and puffed smoke at him. He couldn't stop her from refilling her closet.

He coughed. She reached for a book, and he swiped at her hand with his glowing stick. She snatched her hand back, and he stepped onto the books like he didn't care if he hurt them. *Fiend!*

She ducked sideways.

He blocked her.

She tried another way.

He was in her way again.

Mim's spark faded, and her hearts fluttered. She couldn't rebuild her nest with him in the way.

Across the room, she glimpsed an open window, the curtain rustling in the cool night air, those scents of flowers, cars, and worms filling her again. She had a straight line to it, past the end of the bed.

Outside. Those mysterious scents. Calling her. Tempting her.

She jumped for it. Around the horrible boy with his surprised face. Onto the bouncer that the horrible boy called a trampoline. Bouncing from it into the larger boy's blanket nest, where she collected a pillow and a sock to fill a new nest. Climbing over the bed, where she picked up a random book from the end of it.

She was a rebel! A triumph! She was terrified.

"It's at the window," the horrible boy screamed.

Mim leaped over the ledge. She hit the screen with her too-big horns and busted through. She sailed into the air under a starry sky, falling, falling down, landing with her haunches thumping onto the pillow, rolling onto the cool grass, light spilling from the high-up window.

Outside! She was outside.

The breeze tickled her scales and ruffled her fur, hurling more scents her way. One of her hearts rejoiced to be free, while her other one tugged to be back in her closet.

She might grow as big as the world now. Would she grow to grotesque heights?

Oh, the world was huge. It stretched out forever in all directions. It was dizzying.

"Is it hurt?" the larger boy called from inside.

The horrible boy appeared at the window. "Too dark to see!"

In a lower window, a light blasted on.

Mim gathered her pillow, sock, and book. Then she ran into the wide world.

Chapter 9

Dawz stood with the others in a pool of streetlight on his front lawn. He'd forgotten his coat, but that wasn't why he was shivering. Shadows loomed beyond their circle. Anything could be hiding there, ready to attack.

Seconds after the monster crashed through the window screen, Pop had burst into Dawz's room. He had made sure Dawz and Atlas were okay, then started making calls. He phoned his friend Officer Rashmi. A pest-control guy. And Atlas's mom Thea. Next, he'd woken Jayla, who could sleep through a jackhammer busting through their sidewalk, and rushed them all outside. "No one goes back in for anything," he'd said. "Not until we know it's safe."

Safe. Dawz doubted he'd ever feel safe again.

It took him a moment to realize that Pop hadn't asked what had broken through the window screen.

Like he didn't need to ask.

Now they were gathered outside, under the streetlight, all in their pajamas, with Atlas wide-eyed, Pop tight-lipped and corralling them into a knot, and Jayla talking and talking. "What happened? Why are we outside? Who broke Dawz's screen?"

But Dawz didn't answer her, and Pop still didn't ask.

Officer Rashmi arrived in her police car first. She was a frequent visitor to Pop's kitchen, and not only to sample Pop's food. Dawz had often walked in on them whispering across the kitchen island, and he'd wondered how they'd become friends and why Officer Rashmi always came in uniform. Maybe she was just formal?

Next to arrive was a white guy in a pest-control van and, finally, Thea on her electric bike. Soon, everyone was talking at once. When the pest-control guy disappeared into the house with Officer Rashmi, Dawz knew they wouldn't find anything. The prickle at the edge of his left eye told him the danger was outside, somewhere in the shadows, not inside.

"A monster!" The words burst out of him. "It was a monster."

Everyone went silent, even Jayla, and it unnerved Dawz. Of course, Atlas already knew about the monster, and he spoke first.

"I couldn't see it." Atlas was breathless. "But something unlocked the closet door and busted through the screen. It even stole my sock and Dawz's pillow and book. I could see the things it took."

Dawz had never been so grateful for his friend. His words made Dawz feel less alone. Someone else had witnessed evidence of this monster. But then, Dawz saw Pop's eyes, blue and sad, as if he'd known Dawz was going to say it was a monster and wished he hadn't.

A sinking feeling took over Dawz like dishwater disappearing down a drain, and all he could think was, *If only I'd had a stronger lock. If only I hadn't let the monster escape.*

If only he could turn back time like a character in a book and force it to stay in the closet.

"Cool!" Jayla said. "What did this monster look like?"

Thea made a *tsk* sound. "This town has monsters on the brain. It could have been a raccoon who got in through the eaves."

Before Dawz could argue with her—explain the danger they were in—Officer Rashmi emerged from the house with the pest-control guy, both of them hurrying toward the pool of light.

"All clear." Officer Rashmi nodded to Pop, who nodded back like they'd done this before.

All clear. Suddenly, Dawz remembered a conversation he'd overheard between them. Late one night, when Dawz had come downstairs for a glass of water, Officer Rashmi and Pop had been sipping chai and sampling samosas in the kitchen.

"And that's all you know? No one's seen her?" Pop had whispered.

"It was all clear," Officer Rashmi whispered back. Then her brown eyes locked onto Dawz in the doorway and her voice got louder. "These samosas are as good as the ones my mother used to make in Mumbai. Now, that's hard to do."

Dawz's insides bubbled into lava. Had Pop been

secretly searching for Mom? Did he want her to come back? What would happen to Dawz and Jayla if she did?

"Yep, nothing in that closet anymore," the pest-control guy said. "Didn't even see any scat." His name badge on his jacket read *Ronny*. His logo read *Hug-a-Bug Pest Control*.

"What's scat?" Jayla had brought a flashlight outside with her, which she was beaming into the shadows.

"It's poop," Atlas told her.

"And the rest of the place? You checked it all?" Pop glanced nervously at the house.

"Nothing nowhere, except what should be inside there. What did you see, lads?" Ronny turned to Dawz and Atlas.

"My brother saw a real, live monster, and now she's on the loose," Jayla said. "We should hunt for her. We should learn everything about her." She brandished her flashlight.

The adults exchanged a look that Dawz couldn't read because Jayla had chosen that moment to blind him with light.

He grabbed the flashlight. "How would you know it's a *she*?" Jayla had a habit of calling everything a *she*, which was fine for toys, but now she was making him wonder if the monster might be a *she*, and he didn't want to—he couldn't—think about the monster as anything but an *it*.

"Hey!" Jayla snatched the light back.

"No one is hunting anything." Pop took the light and turned it off. When Jayla reached for it, he shoved it deep in his pocket.

"That's for sure." Thea nodded.

"Except me." Officer Rashmi flipped open the notepad she'd been carrying. Her belt had a scary amount of equipment on it, including handcuffs and a baton. "If a monster is out there, we'll find it."

"What did this monster look like?" Ronny asked.

"Why does everyone keep calling it a monster?" Thea said. "It could have been a—"

"Mom!" Atlas frowned.

"If you'd grown up here, you wouldn't say that." Dawz raised his voice. Who could ignore the howls that echoed across the forest and marsh at night? Or the feeling of being watched from a closet?

An awkward silence grew, and Pop shot Dawz a disappointed look.

"Sorry, Thea," Dawz muttered. "I didn't mean to yell."

"You've been through a lot." Her voice softened. "Just try to keep an open mind. The monster stories in this town may be good for tourism, but that's about it."

Dawz bit his lip to stop himself from talking back.

"What did you see? I'll need a thorough description." Officer Rashmi held her pen above her pad.

Dawz's running shoes sank deeper into the rain-soaked grass. He was the only one who could describe the monster. The only one. "It was shorter than Jayla, but with horns—"

"Cool!" Jayla bounced on her toes.

"How many? What shape?" Ronny asked, like he believed Dawz.

Dawz didn't want to say because Pop had paled and turned away, but Ronny was waiting for an answer. "Two. Curved and pointed. And a gray, furry head like a musk ox."

"Musk ox! We don't get them this far south. Are you sure?"

Dawz nodded. He wasn't sure of much, but he knew what he'd seen. Even though he'd been terrified, he'd memorized everything, like a good cryptozoologist. "It had hands with claws, arms, and a chest like a person, but they were covered in purple scales like a snake. Then its legs were like a musk ox again, but with sharp hooves. The worst part was those creepy glowing eyes on either side of its head."

Officer Rashmi recorded every detail as if it might mean something. Pop crossed his arms over his skinny chest, his eyes locked onto Dawz's bedroom window.

"It's best if you keep as close to the truth as possible," Thea interrupted.

Atlas let out a grunt, followed by a headshake.

"But I am!" Dawz shot his friend a frustrated look, and he shot one right back. He turned to Pop, wanting to break his intense stare. "You believe me, right?" He wished Pop would say something to stop Thea from interrupting.

Pop ruffled Dawz's hair. "No reason not to." His forced smile left Dawz feeling hollow.

"Listen, lad," Ronny began. "I once got a call from a guy who claimed to see a cross between a wasp and a rat. By the time I got there, it was gone. Same with the time I got a call to rid a yard of fairies. Can you believe it? Fairies!" He snorted.

"This was nothing like that." Dawz frowned. Was this man making fun of him?

"But I've also seen things I never thought possible. One family had a colony of bats roosting in their attic.

The bat droppings were over two feet high in spots. One bat was as big as a mini-pterodactyl!"

"Wow!" Jayla said. "I'd like to see that."

"Yup, it was impressive. Another time, I treated a house with hundreds of garter snakes crawling in the walls. But the worst was a call to a cabin where a guy claimed he saw a wolf that was bigger than a human."

"I've heard about wolves like that," Atlas said.

Thea frowned. "Those are just stories."

"Are they, ma'am?" Ronny stared her down, even though she was as wide as Atlas, and Dawz began to like this man. "Now, gray wolves can grow bigger than six feet, but this laddie was over seven or my name isn't Ronny McCoy. That beast turned toward me, and there was a man's face where his snout should've been! I wouldn't have believed it if I didn't see it with my own eyes."

"I want to be a pest controller when I grow up," Jayla announced.

"I don't." The words popped out before Dawz could stop them.

"So you'll be patrolling for this thing?" Pop asked Officer Rashmi.

She nodded. "We'll have cars sweeping the area." She began explaining her plan to Pop and Thea, turning to gesture at the town.

Only in Morsh, thought Dawz. In the city, most people would think like Thea, and no cops would search for a monster reported by a boy.

Meanwhile, Ronny leaned down to Dawz and Atlas.

"I wasn't trying to scare you lads," he said.

53

"We're not scared," Dawz lied.

"I'm just saying that some creatures *are* monsters, and Morsh seems to be sitting in a place where that happens more often than not."

"Why?" asked Jayla.

Ronny shrugged. "Maybe we're closer to the crust of the spirit world, where different types of creatures get tangled together on the way into life. I don't know, but I'm just telling you that I promise to keep an eye out for this monster. Chances are it'll be looking for a new place to nest. And when I hear about it, I'll root it out."

"I can help," Jayla said.

Atlas gave her a playful shove that meant *Let Ronny take care of it.*

"You could report any sightings," Ronny suggested.

"Thanks." Dawz felt better with Ronny on the case. At least he believed him. Not like Thea, who didn't understand that Dawz *was* telling the truth. But he didn't like the idea of Morsh sitting close to the spirit world. What was that supposed to mean? He tried not to think about it. "What do you do with the creatures, once you catch them?"

"I'm a catch-and-release guy." Ronny stuck his thumbs in his belt loops. "I drive them into the forest and set them up in a new place."

"Even monsters?" Jayla asked.

"Even monsters need a place to live. Just maybe not in your brother's closet, huh?" Ronny grinned wide enough to show his crooked teeth.

"Do they ever come back?" Dawz asked. "After you release them?"

"Not if I take them far enough. And don't you worry. I'll make sure this monster doesn't bother you again."

Dawz liked the way Ronny's grin spread across his face and into his eyes. Maybe Ronny or Officer Rashmi would be able to find this monster. "Maybe it should be locked up," he suggested.

Ronny studied Dawz, and his grin faded. "If it's that bad, I may need to."

Soon Pop was shaking hands with Officer Rashmi, then Ronny was handing Pop a bill. "Thanks for everything," Pop said. "Come by sometime, and I'll make you a meal."

"Sure thing," Ronny said. "Call if you need anything else."

"Come on, Jordy," said Thea, who still called Atlas by his real name. "Get your bike and let's go home."

"But it's a sleepover—"

"We've had enough excitement for tonight."

"That's for sure." Pop tugged Jayla and Dawz closer.

Jayla pulled away but Dawz tucked in. How was he ever going to fall asleep tonight? He missed Atlas already.

Atlas and Thea cycled away. Ronny rattled off in his van, followed by Officer Rashmi in her car. Even though Pop was right beside Dawz, the shadows tucked closer too.

Chapter 10

Mim ran, hugging her book, pillow, and sock with one arm and pumping with the other, pressing off with her hooves, carrying herself away from the horrible boy, feeling the wide world whooshing by in waves that threatened to drown her.

Waves of buildings—too many to count.

Waves of smells—human and not.

Waves of light—blasting from high-up poles, the front of cars, and buildings, always buildings. She knew buildings had closets in them, but her feet wouldn't stop running long enough to find one.

Mim gulped one breath after another, but she couldn't get enough air. She sensed the horrible boy at her back, although she couldn't see him anywhere when she turned around.

Her hooves clomped on the hard road, each step jarring her teeth, her head, her bones until a rattle filled her. *Tat-a-tat-a-tat!*

Then, from nowhere, a human appeared in her path, along with a fur beast that Mim thought might be a friend because he wagged his tail—right before he yipped and yapped at her. Loud. With pointed teeth.

Mim squealed, accidentally dropping her book, pillow, and sock. *Dog.* She remembered the word *dog*, but *fur beast* seemed like a better name.

"Shush!" The human yanked at a rope attached around the fur beast's neck. "It's only an old pillow. Nothing to bark at."

Nothing! Mim was not nothing. She panted and hissed as the human and barking fur beast passed, then she collected her things and ran on, veering onto the grass. Her hooves sank with each step. Into a ditch. Splashing through water. Between two buildings. Into the comfort of shadows.

So far, only the horrible boy and the nasty fur beast had seen her, although everyone seemed to be able to see her pillow. She didn't want to be seen by either creature, yet to be unseen by others made her feel like she didn't exist. But she did. She did.

Couldn't she feel her legs begging to stop running? Couldn't she feel her chest burning with each breath? Couldn't she hear the roar of the wide, wide world?

When her legs said, *No more*, and her chest said, *I can't*, Mim stopped and the world stilled too.

She stood in a not-wide street, breathless and glancing around and above her. The street had settled between a row of unlit buildings on one side and a fence that kept out tall trees and more buildings on the other side. No humans in sight. No lights on poles.

But she needed a nest. A small one. Where could she find small?

Mim squeezed into a sliver of space between a brick wall and a large metal bin that smelled of human food and rot, metal foil and soiled cardboard. It wasn't a comforting smell like dust and dry floorboards, but it didn't smell like boy either. The space was nicely narrow although too high up to a sky that was star-filled and terrifyingly huge.

She clutched her book, pillow, and sock, and tried to catch her breath. She hoped she wouldn't grow up to the sky like a skinny tree.

Mim needed smaller. Much smaller.

"Raar," said a new fur beast.

Mim jolted upright, nail-claws out.

The fur beast stood on four legs a short distance away. While Mim trembled, the fur beast mewed, raared, and sniffed at her a few times before turning in a circle, exposing her back to attack. Then the fur beast sat down, curled her skinny tail around herself, and licked one paw thoroughly clean.

What mischief is this?

The fur beast was orange with white stripes and golden eyes that locked onto Mim, clearly seeing her. As Mim worried, the beast cleaned both front paws, then her ears, finally releasing her eye-lock on Mim.

Mim's arms and hands tired from holding her nail-claws ready, and she slowly lowered them. This fur beast was grooming. Mim used to rub her scales against the brick wall in her closet to clean off dust balls. Grooming meant the fur beast was comfortable.

"Raar," said the fur beast once again and then once more, and Mim decided to name her Raar. Maybe it was the fur beast's name for herself.

Then Raar stood, and Mim stiffened. Raar walked right up to Mim, nudged the pillow out of the way, and rubbed against Mim's legs. A rumble as loud as a car began deep inside Raar, and Mim wondered at it, wishing she could rumble too, gentle yet fierce. How did Raar make that rumble sound?

Mim reached out, slow and careful.

She touched the fur beast, marveling how the rumble traveled through Raar's silky fur and into the palm of her own hand. She stroked the fur—softer than soft, silkier than the wiry tufts between Mim's horns—and Raar rumbled louder. Mim thought about the other nasty fur beast with the pointed teeth. He wasn't a friend.

Was Raar a friend?

Yes. Mim smiled. *This must be a friend.*

A friend who might be able to make a book work.

Raar rumbled and rumbled. Mim stroked her, wondering why fur beasts could see her and humans couldn't—other than the horrible boy. Just thinking about him made Mim shudder. She hoped she never saw him again.

Mim wiggled her book out from under the pillow, where it had fallen. Raar stopped rumbling. The book had pictures of pleasantly fearsome creatures on the cover—she liked the one with tentacles best. Mim thought of the story friends she'd left behind in the horrible boy's room. Never again would Mim hear the boy's grown-up make a book work. If she wanted story friends to come out and play, she would have to do it herself, with her new friend.

Mim opened her book. Raar stood up and wandered away.

"Friend?" Mim called. She hadn't spoken in a while, so her voice wasn't sure how to work.

Raar disappeared around the corner of the bin.

"Friend!" Mim shouted.

She couldn't lose her. Not so soon. Not now.

Mim shoved her book and her sock into her pillowcase beside her pillow. She couldn't lose them either, especially her book. Then she slung her pillowcase of things over her back and followed Raar.

The orange-and-white fur beast walked down the middle of the not-wide street. Mim slinked from shadow to shadow, wary of threats.

When Raar ducked into a doorway, Mim followed. Raar circled around and around, raaring and glancing at the door as if she wanted to go into the building.

Mim smelled for any signs of humans beyond the door, but she could only catch a sugary scent with a pleasant tang. She worried if the building would be safe, but she trusted Raar.

Mim turned the knob. The door didn't open. She poked at the lock, but it was too small to fit her newly grown nail-claw.

Raar growled in her throat and padded to a pile of boxes. Mim wondered if one of those would make a good nest for them both, but Raar climbed the boxes to a high-up window that was slightly open.

Clever friend!

Raar nudged the window open with her nose and stepped onto the ledge, pausing only to give Mim a look that said *Are you coming, friend?*

"Yes, I am!" Mim hurried up the pile of boxes, which wobbled under her weight. But Mim knew boxes as well as she knew her closet, and soon she'd squeezed onto the ledge next to Raar, who pawed at a screen that blocked them, pushing it inward with an expert swipe.

The sugary tang grew stronger. It was a friendly scent that reminded Mim of home. She caught the faint odor of humans too, but none nearby.

Raar entered the building first, and Mim pulled her pillowcase full of things after her.

Raar didn't explore the room. She headed for a cushion on the floor by the door to the not-wide street. Beside it sat a water bowl and another bowl with nasty-smelling meat in it. Raar began to eat steadily.

A nest! Raar had brought Mim to her nest. *What an honor. What luck.*

Even though Raar's nest was too open, Mim sat on the cushion. It smelled like Raar, and her fur was on it.

It was a good nest, but not for Mim. She glanced around, quickly finding a cupboard she could open. It was near Raar's nest, and delightfully small. Mim emptied the cupboard. Large silver bowls clanged onto the floor. Then she climbed inside and tugged her pillowcase full of things after her.

"Raar?" she called.

She hoped Raar would nest in the cupboard too,

but she understood if Raar preferred her cushion nest. Everyone needed to nest in their own way.

Mim pulled out her book in case Raar joined her. If only they could make the book work soon. Mim wanted to learn how to create story friends, but she also wanted the power to tame dangerous creatures she might meet in this wide world. Mim clutched her book and rested her head on her pillow, suddenly exhausted. The sugary-tang scent of her new nest felt comforting. This nest was the right size, without much extra space. She was certain it would keep her from growing.

Mim listened to Raar crunching her food. She missed the sound of the horrible boy murmuring in his sleep and how she could startle him awake by crashing books. Still, this nest had to be better than her closet nest. Also, this nest had Raar, and Mim couldn't wait to try the book together.

Chapter 11

Dawz woke to the sound of a monster screaming. It took him a while to realize that the scream was coming from his own throat.

His legs were tangled in his blanket. Sweat drenched his sheets. Light from the streetlamp chased nighttime shadows into the corners of his bedroom. A lump rose from the floor, making Dawz sit up and press against his headboard, until he realized that it was Atlas's empty sleeping bag.

A dream lurked, confusing him. Monsters had been coming to get him. Dawz glanced at his clock—3:12 a.m.—and tried to breathe slowly, just as the door to his bedroom burst open and Pop barreled into the center of the room. He wore polka-dot pajama shorts and a T-shirt, and he brandished a silver pancake flipper like a weapon.

"Where is it? Are you okay?" Pop's eyes were wide and darting from Dawz to the shadows, and his skinny arm shook.

Panic swamped Dawz. "It came back?" His voice came out rough, his throat sore from screaming. "Where is it? Do you see it?"

He picked up the lightsaber that he'd left beside his bed and switched it on. It bathed his room in cool blue light. He didn't feel a prickle at the edge of his left eye, so he wasn't sure where to aim. He swung the saber back and forth, but that only made shadows lurch around his bed.

Suddenly, the ceiling light blazed on, and Dawz squinted, breathing hard. Jayla stood in his doorway, hand on the light switch, her hair messy and her pajamas rumpled.

"Am I too late?" She blinked, then rubbed one eye. "I don't want to miss the monster again."

Dawz scanned the room, grateful for the light, grateful he could see no monsters—yet. He jumped out of the bed and checked under it. Nothing. He hurried to the bedroom closet and tugged on the doorknob. Still locked. He turned in a slow circle, examining all corners of his room. Still nothing.

When he was certain the monster had only been in his dream, he turned off his lightsaber, embarrassed that he'd been screaming loud enough to wake even Jayla. It must have been piercing.

"Sorry." Dawz ducked his head. "I had a bad dream."

His dream came back to him like a flood springing from the marsh. His closet had become a doorway to the spirit world, spewing out hideous monsters that were twisted parts of humans and beasts for him to battle all by himself. No Atlas. No Pop. No Jayla. He had barricaded the closet door with his bed, dresser, and anything else he could find, but the monsters had burst through, breathing fire that had set his room ablaze, surrounding him in flames that closed in, tighter and tighter.

"Then you're okay?" Pop's voice shook, and Dawz glanced at him, then wished he hadn't. Pop's face had a guarded, nervous look that made Dawz nervous too.

"Just a dream." Dawz went back to bed with his lightsaber, willing them to leave his room. He didn't want Pop to think something was wrong with him. That the wrongness might get too big to handle. That it might ruin everything. Mom had ruined everything. He had to be more like Pop.

"If you're sure." Pop turned from Dawz without giving him a hug. He switched off the overhead light and took Jayla by the hand.

"Why do I have to sleep in my own room?" Jayla whined. "Why can't I sleep here?"

Dawz's bedroom door clicked shut. The shadows grew. He pulled the blanket over his head and tried to sleep, but it was impossible. He listened to rain batter the roof and worried about the shadows until the morning light began to brighten his room.

A new dream came to haunt him then. Mom had suddenly returned after so many years, driving into Morsh in her same rusted blue car. She collected Dawz and Jayla like leftover luggage, even though Dawz begged her to let him stay. Jayla was excited to go. Pop didn't object, even though he'd adopted them. He just let Mom drive them away from Morsh, heading back to the city. Trees whizzed by. The town retreated. Dawz felt smaller and smaller as he got farther from Morsh, Pop, and his kitchen.

He woke to blinding sunlight, wondering if Pop would miss him.

Dawz dressed quickly. On the stairs, muffled voices and the nutty scent of oatmeal with maple syrup drifted up from the kitchen. As he entered, he found Jayla, Pop, and Officer Rashmi sitting together at the island.

Pop jumped up with a guilty look on his face. He was already wearing his apron and Bakers' Brawl hat. "Take my seat," he said, even though the chair beside Officer Rashmi sat empty.

They must have been talking about him. A sharp pain tightened Dawz's chest.

"I'm fine," he said, his voice still rough. He served himself some oatmeal and leaned against the counter to eat it.

The first bite was warm and soothing. Pop really was a kitchen wizard. Even though he was still giving Dawz that guarded, nervous look, Pop's oatmeal filled Dawz up.

"Any news?" Dawz asked Officer Rashmi, trying to keep his voice casual. She was in uniform, as usual.

She shook her head, swallowing the last of her oatmeal. "I was just saying that we've had no sightings yet."

Yet. Dawz wondered how many other townsfolk received personal case reports over breakfast. He wondered what secrets Pop and Officer Rashmi had shared in this kitchen.

"If we're lucky, the monster will come back," Jayla said with her mouth full.

Dawz shook his head, steadily eating his oatmeal while Jayla rambled on about how much she wanted to see a monster. When he was done, he put his bowl and spoon in the dishwasher, then stepped into the hall to grab his bike helmet from the closet.

"Where are you going?" Pop's voice came from behind him, making Dawz jump.

"Atlas's place, remember? We always practice baking on Sundays." Less than a week until the Bakers' Brawl, and baking felt like the most normal thing Dawz could do after seeing a monster last night.

"I should drive you." Pop reached for the keys on the hook beside the front door.

"I can bike. You stay here."

"But—"

"I'm fine," Dawz said, even though he wasn't. He really wasn't.

"Are you sure?" Pop followed him onto the front porch, still with that look on his face. Dawz couldn't tell if he was concerned or disgusted, and he wasn't going to ask.

"I'm sure."

"All right." Pop hugged him, but it was an uneasy one. "Call as soon as you get there."

"I will."

When Dawz finally pulled away on his bike, he felt relieved. He swerved around puddles from last night's rain. He pedaled hard to get up the hill on their road. He turned the corner toward Main Street and Atlas's place. His legs were tired already. His bike wobbled as he scanned the passing ditches and lawns too. Morning mist hovered in the hollows, making it hard to see if anything was hiding. The sun peeked from behind a cloud, then darted back in, as if it couldn't decide what to do.

Where was the monster now? Had it run all the way out of town? Had Ronny caught it? If only.

Dawz just wanted to have a day with no monsters in it. He wanted to practice for the Bakers' Brawl with Atlas. He wanted to find a way to win this year's contest. He needed a win more than ever.

Chapter 12

Mim woke to the sound of a human voice.

"What the—" the voice said.

She jerked upright, banging the side of her head against the top of the cupboard and startling Raar, who had been snuggled against her and the book.

"Who dumped my bowls on the floor?" the voice said.

Raar recovered from the shock first, yawning and stretching with her haunches in the air, leaving a chill where she'd warmed Mim. She sniffed Mim's book with interest, but how could they make a book work with a human so close? When Raar nudged the cupboard door open with her nose, Mim grabbed for her.

"Not safe," Mim hissed.

But Raar squirmed free and pushed open the door. Daylight beamed in, stinging Mim's eyes and filling them with tears.

"Sparkle!" scolded the voice. "Did you make this mess?"

"Raar," Mim's friend answered. Why would she even raar at this human? Was Sparkle her name?

Mim cowered in the cupboard, worrying for Raar or Sparkle or whatever she'd named herself. What if this human hurt her?

She had to rescue her friend.

Mim wiped her eyes clear and squinted into the light. From her hunched position inside the cupboard, she could see her friend padding around the silver bowls, then weaving between the thick human legs. *Foolish fur beast! Humans cannot be trusted!*

Mim worried the legs might attack Raar-Sparkle. She tucked her book, pillow, and sock into a corner for safekeeping. She squirmed her way out of the cupboard—it felt smaller than before—finally jerking free.

She tumbled onto the hard floor and into a beam of sunlight, smoke snorting from her nostrils. Then she bumped into the human legs with her nail-claws. The tips pierced skin in a way that repulsed Mim, but it also felt right because Raar-Sparkle *needed* her. Instantly, several satisfying dot-shaped welts appeared on the human's leg.

"Ow, Sparkle! Keep your claws to yourself!" the human exclaimed. She didn't seem to notice Mim's puff of smoke, which floated toward her.

Mim shielded her eyes and scuttled backward. The woman was wide, tall, and stupid—another human who couldn't see her—and Mim decided being invisible to most humans wasn't so bad. As the woman reached a hand down, down, down toward

Raar-Sparkle, Mim lunged forward and batted it away with one horn, then readied herself for defense.

"What was that?" The woman pulled her hand back and studied the space where Mim stood.

Mim didn't move, although she wanted to run and hide.

The woman tilted her head and wrinkled her eyebrows. She had a pile of black hair and a moldy scent that screamed danger. Couldn't Raar-Sparkle smell it?

Although she'd never defended for two before, Mim figured she should position herself between Raar-Sparkle and the woman, who was reaching down again. This time, Mim scratched the woman's bare arm with one sharp nail-claw until blood appeared—sickeningly red, not purple like Mim's blood was when she'd cut her finger on a sharp floorboard—and she gagged at the sight of it.

The woman gasped and pulled back, a welt appearing already. "No, Sparkle! No scratching!" She pressed her hand against the wound, probably to slow the disgusting blood. Hopefully, she'd leave them alone now.

Then Raar-Sparkle wove around Mim, heading toward the woman.

No! Mim pulled Raar-Sparkle backward by the tail.

Her friend raared louder than ever, just as the woman's hand reached again. It touched Raar-Sparkle's head. It opened to grab hold of her neck. And it petted.

What strangeness! Mim plopped backward into a large bowl, breathing hard.

"What's got into you? Why are you a bad kitty today?" The woman petted and Raar-Sparkle raared.

"There, there, you wouldn't scratch me again, would you? No, you wouldn't."

How could Raar-Sparkle *like* this woman? Were they *friends*?

Raar-Sparkle let the woman pick her up and cuddle her. Then Mim's friend began to rumble.

A jagged bolt of lightning sparked between Mim's hearts. To watch Raar-Sparkle rumble with the woman the way she'd rumbled with Mim! A rumble that could persuade anyone to be a friend, even a human. Mim sagged deeper into the bowl, hoping she hadn't lost her friend for good.

That couldn't happen. Could it?

The sunlight beamed relentlessly, lighting up Raar-Sparkle's fur like fire, and hurting Mim's eyes more and more. Nest. She needed another nest now. If she found one nearby, then maybe Raar-Sparkle would join her. Maybe Raar-Sparkle would try the book with her.

Mim hauled herself out of the bowl. The room had a long counter with cupboards underneath, where she'd first nested. Opposite it stood a row of gleaming silver appliances that looked too hard to get into. At the far end of the room sat rows of tables and chairs in front of a too-bright window.

She scuttled around the edges of the room, searching the walls for a cubbyhole or closet. The sweet-tangy scent was strongest near the counter. So comforting, so appealing.

Mim inhaled deeply. She followed her snout. But she found no cubbyhole, no closet.

She glanced at Raar-Sparkle, who was still rumbling with the woman instead of Mim. This woman was ruining everything.

"Now, let's get your breakfast," the woman said to Raar-Sparkle.

"Raar," said Raar-Sparkle.

Mim couldn't watch anymore. She circled back to her cupboard and stuck her head inside. She didn't want to leave this nest or her new friend, but the woman was a problem and Mim's back end didn't fit into her cupboard nest as well as it had last night. She was still growing, and she needed a new small nest, with or without her friend. Reluctantly, she packed her book into her pillowcase, checked her sock and pillow were still safely inside, and backed out of her cupboard.

Goodbye, cupboard nest, she thought. Her pillow held the scent of Raar-Sparkle, and it was bittersweet.

The door to the not-wide street was open now, and someone had moved Raar-Sparkle's cushion nest outside, along with her water dish.

Near the counter, Raar-Sparkle was pacing around the woman's feet, raaring loudly. The woman was filling the food dish.

"Just a minute, Sparkle, you impatient one!" the woman scolded again, but Mim could now hear friendship behind the scolding. "Outside with you"—she carried the dish into the not-wide street and set it next to Raar-Sparkle's cushion nest—"or the health inspector will have something to say about how I run my café!"

Raar-Sparkle darted into the street after the woman. Mim followed, pulling her pillowcase behind her.

"Bring your friends next time," the woman told Raar-Sparkle. "I have plenty more."

I'm a friend, Mim thought sadly. But she didn't want to eat the meat-scented food in Raar-Sparkle's bowl. And from the way Raar-Sparkle was gulping it down, she doubted her friend would share.

The woman headed toward the building, tripping over Mim.

"What in the world is this old pillow doing here?" she exclaimed.

Mim gripped her pillowcase of things tighter. The woman picked it up, with Mim attached to it.

"So heavy!" the woman remarked.

It's mine, Mim thought, but she released it, only to scramble after it as the woman lifted it higher and dumped it near Raar-Sparkle's cushion nest, right in a beam of sunlight.

"For your friends," the woman said. Then she went back inside.

Mim was relieved the woman was gone. She scurried to pick up her pillowcase of things, hating how the sunlight heated her skin. She retreated to a shadow to confirm her book and sock were safe inside. Then she explained to Raar-Sparkle that she needed to find a new nest, but Raar-Sparkle didn't seem to listen. Instead, her friend gulped the last of her food, then sauntered to her cushion nest, turned in a circle three times, lay down, and shut her eyes.

"Friend?" Mim ventured into the sunlight to poke Raar-Sparkle.

She opened one eye and shut it again.

"Friend!" Mim's voice trembled.

The sunlight pricked Mim's eyes. She needed shade. She needed small. But her new friend seemed to need the woman's food and this cushion nest in the sun.

With her head heavy, Mim picked up her pillowcase and turned from Raar-Sparkle.

"Goodbye, friend." Mim's nostrils flared. She scooted into the shade of the fence and sniffed the air, wondering which way to go.

A boy appeared at one end of the not-wide street, riding a bike. Mim pressed herself against a fence, instantly tense.

Please don't let it be him. She peeked out.

But it was.

The horrible boy was riding down the not-wide street toward her.

Mim couldn't believe it. Why was he here? Was he following her? She tucked behind a thorny plant, then squeezed between two fence boards. Maybe he would pass by. *Please*, she begged, *let him pass by.*

Chapter 13

When Dawz biked past the corner where the Bear Beast statue stood, he pedaled faster. It always made him anxious, but today he felt more jittery than usual.

The Bear Beast snarled from one of the Four Corners at the center of Morsh, with its back to the large town park and community center that hosted the Bakers' Brawl each year. Shops perched on the other three corners, and the streets were lined with even more stores. Most were closed on Sunday mornings, but not Thea's Café. Atlas and his moms lived above it, with the entrance to their apartment up a set of stairs in the alley.

As he turned into the alley, still biking hard, Dawz's legs were wet spaghetti pushing through jelly. He cycled past the back of the Morsh General Store, with a wooden fence and backyards opposite it. As he got closer to Atlas's, an uncomfortable prickle made him tense. He didn't know how the prickle worked or why it always happened at the edge of his left eye, but he knew he trusted it. Hadn't it warned him about the monster in his closet?

He pedaled slower, scanning side to side for any signs of the monster.

His bike wobbled. He hit a water-filled pothole hard. But he saw no monsters.

The prickle continued as he parked his bike next to the stairs to Atlas's place. The stray cat that Thea fed lay sprawled on a nearby cushion. She meowed and raared when she saw Dawz, leaping up to rub against the legs of his jeans.

"Hey, Sparkle." He patted her, mostly for his own comfort because the prickle still wasn't fading.

She purred against his legs as he scanned for places a monster might hide. The weedy bushes against the fence? *Not enough cover.* The pile of old cardboard boxes, damp from the rain? *Yes.*

He kicked at the bottom box. Sparkle yowled. The pile tumbled.

Dawz jumped back, ready to run if the monster sprang free.

Nothing appeared.

Sparkle retreated to her pillow. Dawz kicked one box and then another. They sounded empty. But he couldn't be sure.

He stomped on one box until it flattened and split. That was better. Then another. Another.

"Dawz?" Atlas watched curiously from his stairs.

Dawz realized he was sweating and breathing hard, but at least the prickle was finally fading to a tingle. He tried to think of a way to joke about the mess around him, but he blurted out, "They were in my way."

Atlas grunted, low and slow, in a way that meant *If you say so.*

Dawz's cheeks heated up. "I'll clean up." He lifted a ripped box, avoiding Atlas's gaze.

"I'll help." Atlas tromped down the stairs, each foot landing with a *thud.*

They leaned the shredded boxes against the wall.

When they were done, Atlas asked, "What should we bake?" They needed to practice different dishes for the Bakers' Brawl because no one knew which Food of Extreme Greatness the judges might ask for.

"Uh, Pizza of Extreme Greatness?" The prickle had left Dawz distracted and uncomfortable. As if the monster might be lurking at the edge of his vision, but he couldn't turn his head fast enough to see it.

Atlas licked his lips. "We can eat it for lunch. Let's get a few ingredients from the café, then we can make it upstairs."

"Okay. But I have to call Pop. He's worried because of the . . ." He didn't want to finish his sentence. Instead, he followed Atlas inside, where he caught a whiff of stale smoke. Had the monster been here? Was that why he'd felt the prickle? Was the monster visiting Dawz's favorite places?

It unsettled him. He was at the center of a storm he couldn't escape.

"A bloody monster in a kid's closet!" a customer was saying to Thea at the checkout counter. He was a tourist in hiking gear with an English accent and a blond mustache. "That's what the news report said. I heard an interview with a pest-control bloke."

"He's talking about Ronny!" Atlas elbowed Dawz, who shrank slightly. He hoped Ronny hadn't mentioned him by name. He didn't want to be known as the boy who'd released a monster. But Ronny wouldn't do that, would he?

"I heard that report too," said Luiza from her usual seat near the window. Luiza had brown skin and lively eyes, and her silver hair caught the morning sunlight. Like always, she'd pinned a button to her shirt that read: *Ask Me About Morsh Monsters.* Thea complained about Luiza's monster stories when she wasn't there, but she could hardly kick a former town councilor out of the café, especially one who entertained the tourists and had the community center named after her.

"Did he find the monster?" Hope crept into Dawz.

"Not yet, but the whole town's on alert." Luiza leaned forward, her eyes shining. "We haven't had a monster since—"

"Now, that's enough." Thea cut off Luiza's story, like usual. She passed a steamy latte and an oversized muffin to the tourist. "It could have been a large alley cat. We have plenty of those. Why, last night, one darn cat got inside again, and I had to clean the mess she left!"

"What did she do?" Dawz worried it might've been worse than a cat.

"Knocked all my bowls onto the floor and made herself a home in my cupboard!" She shook her head and smiled.

Dawz didn't smile.

A cupboard was a lot like a closet.

The tourist looked alarmed. He pointed at Thea's arm. "Did she scratch you? That looks infected."

"Yes, she—oh!" Thea clamped a hand on her arm, but Dawz had already glimpsed a nasty cut. "It wasn't that bad before!"

"How did it happen?" Dawz's stomach lurched. He'd never seen a cut ooze greenish-purple pus before.

"On your leg too!" Atlas stepped toward her, and Dawz saw more dots of pus on her calf.

She waved Atlas away like it was no big deal. "I'll just take care of these. That cat!" She pushed past them, heading for the stairs to the basement. "Jordy, take over for a minute?"

Atlas stepped to the checkout counter as if Thea's scratch meant nothing. "That'll be nine dollars and ninety-five cents, please."

Dawz leaned against the industrial fridge and gripped the handle like it was a lifeline. Was the monster poisonous?

He sank into a swamp of guilt. He was responsible for Thea's injury. He'd caused it by releasing a monster from his closet. Now he had to tell Atlas and Thea that she probably had a monster scratch. He had to make her see a doctor. But what would they think of him?

". . . but my friend could see it. It came from his closet," Atlas was proudly telling the tourist and Luiza, who were eagerly devouring the news. "He's like a real cryptozoologist. I wish I could be—"

"Atlas, shut up!" Dawz meant to nudge Atlas, but he elbowed him hard instead.

Atlas reeled back. The tourist and Luiza stared.

"Sorry!" Dawz wanted to take it back, but he

couldn't. He couldn't wipe the injured look from his friend's face. He couldn't stop the guilt from pulling him under. He couldn't prevent Luiza from blabbering that the monster had come from Dawz's closet. "I just didn't want to tell everyone!"

"Why not? I would."

"Yes, why not?" Luiza echoed.

Dawz ignored her. For once, he wished she didn't share monster stories with the whole town. He wished Thea *had* kicked her out of the café. "Because this is all my fault," he told Atlas. "I think the monster scratched your mom. I think it might be poisonous." Dawz hated the horrified look on Atlas's face. "We have to tell her."

Chapter 14

Sunshine beamed. It reflected off puddles. It glinted through mist. And Mim ran from what she'd seen.

The horrible boy hadn't passed her by. He'd stopped. He'd stopped beside Raar-Sparkle.

Run, Mim had urged her friend, but Raar-Sparkle had leaped up to rub against his legs. Then she'd rumbled.

She'd rumbled with the horrible boy.

Mim's hearts sparked at the memory of it. Was a friend still a friend if she rumbled with an enemy? Mim didn't know. She couldn't know.

She let her legs take over. They carried her farther away from the horrible boy and her confusing friend.

Mim's eyes hurt. Her scales itched. Her head was so hot she was panting, although her feet found relief in the cool puddles. But Mim felt a new thing too. As if her insides were empty and needed to be filled. Like a sickness. Or a hunger?

It couldn't be. Hunger growing inside her as her body grew? Was this empty feeling why humans and fur beasts ate?

Stop it, she told her insides. Food could lead to more growing. She needed small more than she needed food. She was sure of it.

Mim kept to the shade of trees and buildings as much as possible, and she darted across the sunlit roads and sidewalks. More humans were around now—driving in cars and opening doors to buildings—and Mim kept away from them. No one seemed to notice her, although they sometimes glanced at her pillowcase, still packed with her sock, book, and pillow. But if she dropped her things, the humans turned away. This made Mim's invisibility feel like a shield, and she remembered a ghost in a story the grown-up had once shared with the horrible boy. No one had been able to see the ghost, which was a powerful skill if you wanted to sneak past others, but not powerful if you wanted a friend. Mim felt like she didn't belong anywhere or with anyone.

Mim missed Raar-Sparkle and their cupboard nest. Too bad her new nest would be without her confusing friend.

Slowly, Mim grew braver, passing nearer to the stupid humans who couldn't see her, while always watching for signs of attack. None of the humans carried a glowing stick like the horrible boy and his friend had, but she didn't trust them anyway.

The itching under her scales grew worse, and Mim wondered if a soak in a cool puddle would help. She found a deep one at the edge of a quiet road with no humans in sight. It was near a long, low building with plenty of windows, a pleasant garden, and an open field with nets at either end. She set down her pillowcase of things and eased into the puddle. Soon, she was resting on her back, letting the water work between her scales. Then she scratched her back against the rough curb until the pesky itch faded.

Sweet relief. It was almost as good as a closet.

Mim shook off the water and muck. She surveyed her surroundings and raised her snout to scent the air. Friendly trees dotted the grass in front of the building, and a smell from its garden pulled at her. Fresh, sweet, and clean. *Come here*, the smell said. *Don't you want to nest near me?*

That's when she noticed her scales—severed from her! Three of them floating in the puddle, and two more on the curb. Purple, mottled with muck.

Mim was falling apart!

She touched her sides and back where her scales had peeled off. New, tender ones had grown in, bigger than ever. She felt like she was living the chilling snake-beast story she'd heard from the safety of her closet nest. In it, the snake-beast had shed its whole skin to reveal bigger scales underneath.

Mim hugged herself like she could hold back her growth. Gigantic. Her new scales were gigantic. She wanted them to be misfits, but she could feel the itch burning under other smaller scales now too. She needed a nest now more than ever.

Mim gathered up her fallen scales, packed them into her sock, and knotted it. Maybe she could find a way to reattach them after she shrank back to size. She tucked the sock package into her pillowcase and hurried toward the fresh smell.

It belonged to tiny, bell-shaped white flowers that hung from slender stems almost as tall as her knees. They rose above a carpet of wide green leaves, bobbing next to a windowless door into the building. She loved how the tiny flowers had a thunderous scent. She was tempted to roll in them, to carry their scent on her fur and scales, but she didn't want to crush them.

She would nest nearby. She had to. Their scent filled her with hope.

Mim dug into the damp earth next to the flowers and away from the door. She piled the earth in front of the hole, hiding the entrance to her new nest. The smell of worms and shade mingled nicely with the flower scent. She also caught a tangy whiff that she hadn't noticed before, and it reminded her of her sweet closet nest. How she missed it!

The work made her pant more, and she longed to rest. Deeper and deeper she dug, testing the hole every so often to make sure it fit her just right. It had to be tight. It had to keep Mim from growing more.

When the hole fit only Mim and her pillowcase full of things, she tucked herself inside and pulled her things in too. As she lowered her head onto her pillow, she could feel her book underneath her, wanting to be shared with a friend.

Soon, she told it. *I promise to share you soon.*

Mim tried to get comfortable. But her legs ached from running. Her scales itched. Her insides asked to be fed. And her head was full of thoughts of Raar-Sparkle and the horrible boy. Why was Raar-Sparkle friendly with everyone—even him? Why had he appeared in the not-wide street, where Mim was? Did he know how to find her?

She needed to stay alert.

She dug out her book and opened it. Inside, she found crisp white pages with more pictures of pleasantly fearsome creatures, just like on the cover. She also found squiggly black marks. They marched in lines across the page, and they were bent into strange shapes too, just like the marks in the book she'd tried to share with the spider, who hadn't been a friend after all. She wondered if these black marks held magic. If she'd ever unlock the magic to find story friends or ways to tame dangerous creatures like the horrible boy. She wondered if she'd unlock it with Raar-Sparkle.

Mim rested her head, just for a minute, on the book.

Her eyelids grew heavier and heavier. They shut. And she slept.

Chapter 15

Dawz stood across the street from the Bear Beast statue, waiting for Pop to pick him up. The beast's claws glinted, and its fangs did too. He couldn't keep his eyes off them.

Behind him, the café was locked and unlit. Thea had finally agreed to go to a doctor, although she hadn't believed for one second that a monster from Dawz's closet might have scratched and poisoned her. But Atlas had believed, and he was as scared as Dawz. What if she got sick and died? Dawz couldn't think about it.

Then Atlas had wanted to go with Thea, and they'd all agreed that Dawz should call Pop for a ride home, even though he had his bike. He hated telling Pop how the monster from his closet had caused more problems. He hated that Luiza had insisted on waiting with him.

"What did the monster look like?" Luiza asked in the rich, booming voice she used for storytelling—a voice that Dawz usually liked, except that today it made everyone on the sidewalk glance at them.

Dawz edged away, pretending she wasn't talking to him. He knew it was rude, but he didn't want to discuss the monster again. The conversation in the café had been bad enough.

"Would you be willing to describe it for a police sketch artist?" Luiza ambled closer, still talking too loud. "It would be useful to know what we're up against. We don't want anyone else hurt."

Dawz hung his head. He wished it was yesterday, when his life had been normal, when his biggest worry was how to make Food of Extreme Greatness with Atlas. Poutine pizza with chocolate gravy. Pickle-and-lollipop cookies. But Luiza was right. He had to warn people, and she was the perfect person to do that for him.

Dawz leaned toward her and described the monster in a quiet voice, hoping only she could hear. But she kept asking loud questions, and his words were like magnets, slowly attracting a crowd. First a few tourists, then some kids from his school, then more and more people stopping to listen, eyes widening.

"A monster? Here?" asked a freckled tourist from under a floppy hat. Her smile annoyed Dawz. He wasn't just telling a scary story.

"So you had a poisonous monster in your closet," said a bossy older girl from Dawz's school. "Why did you let it out?"

"I didn't mean to!" Dawz raised his voice. The tourist with the floppy hat frowned. The bossy girl looked down her nose at him.

"Leave him be." Luiza's tone was sharp. "A monster can be hard for anyone to deal with."

Dawz shoved his hands in his pockets. But it wasn't anyone. It was him.

"I . . . uh . . . need to go." He backed away, avoiding everyone's eyes. He'd warned them. That was enough. Maybe he should ride to meet Pop, but he didn't want to go into the alley alone to get his bike.

"What about the sketch artist?" Luiza asked. "I can set that up for you."

Pop's pickup truck finally turned the corner. Dawz glimpsed his worried face and Jayla's curious one through the windshield.

"Maybe later. My pop's here. I have to go." Dawz fled across the street.

Luiza called after him, and the bossy girl's eyes bored into his back. Meanwhile, Pop parked the truck and leaped out. Jayla leaned out the passenger-side window, waving and making a scene.

"We came to pick you up!" she called.

Pop hugged Dawz like he was a little kid. "I can't believe the monster was in Thea's Café! I should've driven you this morning."

Dawz squirmed free, not wanting the crowd of people to see them hugging. "I'm okay."

"I hope Thea is too." Pop glanced across the street. "What did Luiza want?"

"She had questions. A lot of questions."

Pop shook his head. "She can get a little pushy."

Dawz nodded. He felt guilty for not agreeing to the

police sketch artist, but how would it help if no one else could see the monster? At least he'd given Officer Rashmi a description and warned Luiza that it may be poisonous. He could count on them to spread the news. "When will we hear about Thea?"

"She promised to call after she's done at the clinic. Come on. Let's go home. I'll make us hot chocolate and we can talk."

The serious look on Pop's face made Dawz stiffen. "About what?"

"Something I should have told you both long ago."

Jayla stuck her head out Pop's window. "Mmm, I love hot chocolate!"

Dawz could feel bad news lurking behind Pop's words. "Is it about Mom?" Pop saved that serious look for talks about her. Everyone did. She inspired serious talks, and Dawz hated them. He suspected Pop did too, since he'd told Dawz that he didn't ever have to talk about Mom if he didn't want to. And Dawz hadn't, even with Atlas.

"How'd you guess?" Pop gave him a probing look.

"Just lucky," Dawz said, although he felt anything but lucky.

"I'm lucky at guessing too," Jayla added. "Right now, I'm guessing that my hot chocolate will be loaded with marshmallows."

"Probably." Pop's smile was stiff.

"I just need to get my bike from the alley first," Dawz said. "Can you come with me?"

"I can." Jayla burst out of the truck.

"Sure." Pop rested a hand on his shoulder, and Dawz let it stay there until the three of them reached his bike, partly because the crowd had broken up and partly because he needed strength for the talk.

Dawz hunched over his steamy hot chocolate. Pop and Jayla already had foamy milk mustaches, but Dawz let his mug sit untouched. His stomach couldn't handle anything right now.

Even though the three of them had sat in the same chairs at the island counter a thousand times, the kitchen didn't feel safe. Not like before. Like the day they'd celebrated the signed adoption papers, when Pop officially became their father instead of their uncle. Dawz had been eight, Jayla had been five, and Dawz had finally felt like he had a home where he could belong. That had been a good day, when nothing weird had happened. But today Dawz felt as if something could creep into the kitchen—maybe slither under a locked door or drift right through a brick wall.

"Why aren't you drinking?" Pop asked him. "Is it too sweet?"

"It's creamy and delicious." Even Pop's best hot chocolate couldn't soothe Dawz. "I just . . . can't." He pushed his mug away. Now that he knew the talk was coming, he wanted to get it over with. How bad would it be?

"I'll drink his." Jayla reached for it.

Pop put a hand over hers. "One is enough."

"What did you want to tell us?" Dawz had waited for the milk to heat, for the chocolate to melt, for the marshmallows to be shared.

Pop wiped off his milk mustache and stared into his mug. "You were four and Jayla was one when your mom left you both with me. Do you remember any of it?"

"I remember Mom kissed me goodbye," Jayla said.

Dawz knew she was pretending to remember, and it bugged him because she made Mom sound better than she was.

"Right." Pop squeezed her hand. "And you, Dawz?"

He thought back, even though he didn't want to, focusing on real memories, not invented ones like Jayla did. He didn't want to share the bad stuff with Jayla because it would hurt her like it hurt him, but he couldn't pretend either. "Mom drove away in a blue car. There was a lot of stuff in the back seat."

"Yes."

Dawz remembered how he'd clung to Pop as Mom left, hoping he'd get to stay a long time. How she hadn't looked back or waved. No goodbye kisses, although he wouldn't tell Jayla that. No hugs either. "You held Jayla. I asked how long we could stay."

"You did."

"And you said you didn't know."

"I didn't."

She wasn't coming back after all this time, was she?

Dawz's hands became fists under the table. Maybe his dream had been a warning. Would he and Jayla have to live with her? Would Pop have to give them up?

"Will she come back soon?" Jayla said, echoing Dawz's thoughts. She rocked back and forth in her chair, faster and faster.

"No. I don't think so." Pop sighed. Jayla stopped rocking. Dawz relaxed his fists. "That day, your mom asked me to take care of you both for as long as it took. Her car was packed with camping gear, binoculars, traps . . ." Pop ran his hands over his face and through his long hair. "She was talking wild, and I didn't know what to do."

Dawz braced himself, wondering if Pop had heard her going on about yellow feathers and a scorpion tail. Did he know how disturbing she'd become at the end?

"She said . . ." Pop grimaced. "She said she hadn't been happy since she left this town, but it scared her to come back here. She said she'd seen something as a kid here, and she'd always worried it might find her again. And now it had. She said it was a monster."

"No!" Dawz shook his head to banish Pop's words, but they clung like burs.

"Why did she have traps?" Jayla asked.

"She wanted to hunt the monster, and I couldn't talk her out of it." Pop held Jayla's hand. "Apparently, she was the only one who could see it."

"Just like Dawz?" Jayla stared at him.

"Just like Dawz."

Pop's eyes found him too. Dawz couldn't escape. He felt pinned. Cracked open like a boiled lobster claw. Seen in a way that hurt inside his chest. Could Dawz be seeing the same monster Mom had? But she hadn't talked about horns, purple scales, or a musk ox head.

"What happened to Mom?" Jayla asked.

"She never came back. She never called. I reported her missing. Officer Rashmi and her team conducted a huge search. We heard reports of her"—Pop paused like he might say more, then finished quickly—"but we didn't find her."

"So she could still be out there?" Jayla's voice went high and hopeful.

"Maybe. I don't know." Pop pulled Jayla onto his

lap, still watching Dawz. "I just needed to tell you because of what's been happening."

Dawz sat on his hands to stop them from shaking. "Because I'm seeing a monster, just like she did." He *was* weird like Mom. And they all knew it.

Pop nodded, sad and slow. "At first, I wondered if she was imagining the monster. This town is built on monster stories, so maybe one crept into her head? But I've lived here long enough to suspect that some of those stories are real." He rubbed his eyes with his fists. "I just wish she'd told me about it sooner."

"I wish I could see a monster," Jayla said. "I would teach her to be friends—"

"Stop calling it a *her*!" Dawz exploded out of his chair, knocking it backward. He regretted it when Jayla's face fell and Pop looked defeated—as if he'd expected Dawz would disappoint him, like Mom had. "I'm sorry, but . . ." He picked up his chair, wishing he could set everything right. "I guess it could be a *her*, but it could never be a friend." Why did he have to be the one who could see it? What terrible genes had he inherited?

He didn't want to, but he remembered the small apartment in the big city that he and Jayla had once shared with Mom. The time Mom left Dawz alone with his sister for two forever-long days. How Jayla wouldn't stop crying to get out of her crib. How he knocked it over to free her. How her tears stopped as she crawled out. How he fed her cereal from the low cupboard he could reach and distracted her with the pictures in books, since he couldn't read the words yet. How she fell asleep in his lap, but he stayed awake, watching the shadows chase the sunlight across the floor and out of the sky. How Mom had finally come home but in a sour mood that kept him awake at night, listening to her call out in her sleep. How relieved he'd been to visit Pop with Jayla.

"Until someone catches this monster, we need to be careful. No walking or biking to school alone, or anywhere else. No playing outside without me. If you see anything strange, tell me." Pop focused on Dawz. "I lost my sister. I don't want anything to happen to you."

It already has, thought Dawz. The monster in his closet wasn't a fluke. It was here for a reason. It was here because of him.

Chapter 16

Mim didn't know she'd slept through the night and into the next morning. She didn't know her body had grown so much that it had pushed her out of her garden nest. She didn't know that a few purple scales on the back of her neck had peeled off, revealing new scales underneath like oversized teeth.

Now her head, horns and all, rested on her open book. Her furry snout lay turned to the side, exposed to the first rays of morning sun.

Now peeled-off scales lay scattered beside the white flowers who were her only friends—other than Raar-Sparkle, who was too far away to help.

Luckily, Mim was still hidden behind the mound of dirt she'd dug up.

Unluckily, Mim had nested in a schoolyard, where kids were now gathering to play tag or soccer or talk about the first monster sighting in years. Even worse, the horrible boy and his large friend were both students at the school.

Mim slept on. The shock of the wide world, of finding and leaving her first-ever friend, of running more than ever before, had exhausted her.

She didn't hear the kids playing in the schoolyard. She didn't notice the ache of her insides wanting to be filled up. She didn't wake when the horrible boy and the girl locked their bikes to a chain-link fence as their grown-up cycled away.

Mim woke to a harsh and piercing sound, ringing and ringing until her ears ached. She lifted her head, and sunlight blinded her. How had she been pushed out of her earthy nest?

She glanced around for a way to silence the ringing, to find the shadows again. She was horrified to see her freshly severed scales resting on the dirt. Horrified to realize she'd grown even though she'd dug a tight nest. Horrified at the voices of kids shouting to one another, spreading out across the field and in the garden. Horrified that her insides craved the fragrant food sacks each kid carried. Horrified by the scent of the horrible boy, who had met up with his large friend.

Mim got to her feet, her tail twitching. Too many small humans, crowding her garden nest and tempting her with food sacks. She crouched behind her dirt mound, which was hardly enough to cover her now. The white flowers still smelled thunderously fresh, but they no longer filled her with hope. *Great deceivers!* She would never trust white flowers again.

The ringing stopped as suddenly as it had started, and Mim could only wonder where it had come from, why, and when it might happen again.

Meanwhile, the scent of the horrible boy drifted nearer, filling her snout with his sweet but nasty tang, so like the scents that had lured her to her cupboard and garden nests, and she felt the urge to gag. She'd been drawn to the horrible boy's scent without realizing it. How could *he* smell like *home*?

The horrible boy and his friend walked toward the building, closer and closer. Mim stood, not caring if he saw her, scanning for a safe getaway.

The door into the building stood open. *Escape!* Mim scuttled sideways, stepping on the white flowers in her hurry, then burst through the doorway.

"Monster!" shouted the horrible boy. "Monster!"

Voices in the yard echoed the boy's. She spurted into a blindingly sunny room, desperate for a hiding spot, sprinting across a narrow space and slamming snout first into a shelf that appeared out of nowhere, knocking herself flat.

Books tumbled around her. *Books!*

As Mim scrambled to her hooves, her snout throbbing, she couldn't believe what she saw. So many shelves filled with books. She'd never imagined such glory. Maybe her old story friends were hiding within these books. Or she could meet new story friends, if she could make a book work.

This room had the perfect ingredients for building a nest. If only it weren't in such a dangerous spot.

But her very own book! She realized she'd left it outside with her pillow and sock filled with scales. They tugged at her, asking her to come back for them, but the doorway was already swarming with kids and a loud grown-up.

"Everyone back," the grown-up yelled. "Get in your lines! Your lines! Now!" Then she blew a whistle that drilled into Mim's brain.

Mim covered her ears. *Lines?* Were they preparing to attack, like in stories when the human armies formed lines to battle their enemies?

She raced down one aisle of books, away from the whistle and the crowd. When the aisle ended, she turned down the next one. Then another. The shelves were packed tightly, and she was getting nowhere.

Kids yelled from outside. Voices and footsteps trailed her.

Mim pulled books off shelves to slow any followers. She hated how the books clunked to the floor and sprawled open. She hoped they were happy to help her flee the humans.

Mim paused in a nook with a round table surrounded by walls of more and more books. She was panting hard and unsure where to go. This nook, this small nook, would be a good place to build a nest. If only she could . . .

She inhaled deeply.

Boy. She smelled the residue of the horrible boy and his friend. Not a new scent, but days old.

Here! She backed away from two chairs. *They had sat here! With these lovely books!* Had the books revealed their secrets to him?

She glanced at the covers as if they'd betrayed her.

Why was she drawn to places where the horrible boy had been? Why was her most hated human—her curse—always showing up?

The loud woman with the whistle appeared at the end of an aisle of books. "It must be here somewhere." She peered toward Mim, who froze, hoping this grown-up couldn't see her.

Two other grown-ups appeared. A bulky man in a cap started down the aisle, waving a terrifyingly thick bat back and forth in front of him, coming closer with each step. It reminded her of the horrible boy with his glowing stick, only the bat looked much heavier, and it didn't glow.

Mim wailed. It was a new sound for her, but it wanted to be heard and she couldn't stop it. Part moan, part magnificent howl.

The grown-ups didn't seem to notice her wail. They edged closer. The man swung the bat.

"We need to keep the monster here until the police arrive," he said.

"How are we going to do that when we can't see it?" asked the loud woman.

Mim bolted down a nearby aisle in the opposite direction.

She wouldn't be cornered. She couldn't be.

She wove in and around the shelves. When she glimpsed sunlight between the books on yet another shelf, she thought about outside. Maybe she could escape all these humans in the outside.

But Mim didn't know how to get through all these shelves to reach the outside. They reminded her of a maze in a story she'd heard. A maze where a monster had been trapped by tricky humans. That wasn't going to happen to her!

She pushed the sunlit shelf. When it rocked slightly, she pushed more. Soon, it was teetering and then . . . *CRASH!*

Books scattered. Someone in the room yelled. Mim crawled over the pile of books, hating how she bent their pages, to find the door, then the outside.

She shaded her eyes. Her nest. The crushed white flowers. The yard clear of kids. Except two.

The larger boy crouched beside her nest, peering into it like he could unravel her secrets. Beside him stood the horrible boy, clutching her book to his chest. *Her book!*

Mim's scales rippled. *How dare he touch it!* She wailed her new sound, puffing out smoke and ash, then dove for her book.

The horrible boy's face twisted. His eyes bulged.

As Mim reached for her book, she grazed the horrible boy's cheek with a nail-claw before she—*Bam!*—smacked into his shoulder. A jolt shot through her and ignited her insides. It ricocheted between her two hearts. It kindled a spark of memory: the horrible boy only younger, in bed, crying in his sleep, screaming at her, "Go away, go away!" Then the spark exploded into every cell in her body.

Pain ripped through Mim. She could feel herself growing. She could see it too—in her arms, her nail-claws.

She flailed. She fell to the ground and rolled into a ball, desperate to stay small.

But Mim grew and grew.

"Dawz!" shouted the larger boy. "Are you okay?"

The horrible boy—she guessed he'd named himself Dawz—lay a short distance from her. On his side. His cheek bleeding red, disgusting red. Gripping his shoulder with a dazed look on his face. Her book lay between them. He had dropped her book.

"The monster's growing!" Dawz the Horrible said. "Can you see it?"

"No! Where?"

Mim got to her feet, groaning. Her everything hurt. Her nail-claws were twice as long. Hunger howled through her insides, more demanding than ever.

Dawz the Horrible stood too. She'd grown as big as him. In only a moment, Mim had expanded to the size of this boy.

She was ghastly. Vast. More of her too-small scales lay at her feet. Severed.

Mim snatched her book up. The larger boy pointed and gasped.

"The book moved," he yelled.

"Give that back," called Dawz the Horrible. But he didn't reach for it.

Mim's pillowcase and sock sat behind him, and she didn't want to touch him again to get them back. *Goodbye, pillowcase. Goodbye, sock full of scales*, she mourned. Then her hunger made her grab the food sack that the larger boy had dropped.

"It's got my lunch!" The larger boy lunged for it.

"Don't!" Dawz the Horrible pulled him back.

Mim stepped away, stumbling over her too-big hooves. She held the food sack by the strap and hugged her book. She could hear the grown-ups shouting from inside the room of books.

"It's out here!" Dawz the Horrible called. "The monster is here!"

Mim turned and ran, her giant hooves tearing up the spring grass.

Chapter 17

Dawz sat on a bed at the town medical clinic with his arms crossed. He was wearing his favorite T-shirt—the one that read *Demi-God in Training*—but right now it felt like the biggest lie ever. His cheek ached where the monster had sliced him. Even though it had stopped bleeding, it throbbed so much his teeth hurt.

"I don't want to do the tests," he said through the mask Dr. Lin had told him to wear. If only it would cover the gash on his cheek, but that was near his eye and oozing slightly.

"Look, Dawz. We really need to listen to Dr. Lin," Pop said.

Everyone else who'd gathered around Dawz's bed had to wear a mask too, as if he might infect them. Dr. Lin, Pop, and Officer Rashmi all had the same worried eyes above their masks, while Jayla was cornering an imaginary monster between his bed and a table, waving a stick that she'd brought from the schoolyard.

She knocked over a cup of water. It splashed onto Dawz's bed and pooled under his butt. In seconds, he was sitting on a soggy sheet in soaked jeans with Jayla flourishing her stick close to his head.

He grabbed it and snapped it in half.

"You broke my sword!" she yelled.

"Stop waving it in my face!" he yelled back.

"Dawz! Jayla! Please!" Pop took the broken stick and held it up high. "What were you saying, doctor?"

Jayla began karate-chopping the air where her imaginary monster stood. *Monsters aren't a game*, Dawz wanted to say. But Dr. Lin stood next to the bed, waiting to usher him away to be tested and prodded. He already knew he was connected to the monster in some terrible way. He didn't need proof that there was something wrong with him.

"We need to learn what we can about this creature." Dr. Lin frowned down at him. "We'll just need a blood test and a tissue sample from where it scratched your cheek."

"Where it sliced me with its claw, you mean," Dawz said.

No one understood what had happened. When the monster dove at him, a shadow descended too, and it still hovered over him. He didn't want to be the boy who'd made the monster grow. He didn't want to be examined. He wanted to hide under a blanket, but he was too old for that, and the bed only had the thin, soggy sheet.

"That wound from the claw is why you need to do the tests," Pop said. "Please, Dawz."

Dr. Lin nodded. "I'm hoping they'll tell us more

about the toxin on the claws and why the creature grew bigger when you touched it."

"I didn't touch it!" Dawz exploded. "Like I told you, it attacked me!" He wished Atlas was here. He wished someone understood him.

"Yes, we know." Officer Rashmi exchanged a meaningful look with Pop, and Dawz wondered what that meant.

"You have the scales. Can't you test those?" At least everyone could see them. Purple, rough, thick as armor. He wondered why they were visible now. Was it because they were severed from the monster?

"I have a plan to get them tested in the city," said Officer Rashmi. "I'm doing my job. Now it's time to let Dr. Lin do his."

Dawz glared at a disgusting yellow stain on the ceiling. Tests wouldn't tell him anything he didn't already know. The monster's claw had infected him like it had infected Thea—and her wounds were getting worse, even though Dr. Lin was trying. And it was Dawz's fault.

His fault.

His cheek throbbed more than ever. This monster was here for him, or because of him. He might be the only one who *could* do anything about it. Was that why Mom had hunted her monster? Not that he wanted to be anything like her, but how could Ronny or Officer Rashmi catch the monster when they couldn't see it or sense where it was?

"Dawz?" Dr. Lin hovered over him.

"Fine. Whatever." Dawz knew he was being a jerk, but he didn't know how to stop.

"Do you think monsters have best friends?" Jayla appeared from behind Pop, clasping his hand and swinging it. "Do you think they like to play fight?"

"Do you have to interrupt every conversation?" Dawz blurted out.

"Do you have to be so mean?" Jayla snapped back.

"Just go with Dr. Lin, Dawz." Pop shot him a warning look.

"But she always—"

"Go!" Pop raised his voice.

Dawz and Jayla stared. That was new.

"Please." Pop shook like a tree in a breeze. "I need you to do this."

Dawz let Dr. Lin lead him away.

In a lab room, Dr. Lin directed Dawz to a chair. Then he put on gloves before coming anywhere near Dawz.

"I'm not toxic," Dawz grumbled. But he wasn't so sure.

"Gloves are just a precaution." Dr. Lin's voice was muffled by his mask.

He poked a needle into Dawz's arm, and it hurt. Meanwhile, Pop hovered in the hallway, watching through the small window as if Dawz was a little kid who might misbehave. At least Pop had made Jayla stay in the waiting room with the receptionist.

When his blood flowed into the test tube—red, thick, and normal—Dawz felt relieved. But the tissue sample from his cheek oozed hideous greenish-purple goo, just like with Thea. It reminded him that he was sick and wrong. Even when Dr. Lin was bandaging the aching cut on his cheek, he could feel disgusting goo oozing into the gauze.

Dawz slouched in the chair, trying not to think about how much his cheek hurt. He wished he knew some way to stop the monster without hunting it. Maybe he could find its latest hiding spot. Then he could lead Ronny and Officer Rashmi to it. He didn't want to touch it ever again in case he made it grow even bigger, but shouldn't he try to help?

After the bandaging, Dr. Lin told him to wait while he got Dawz some pills and a special cream he made himself.

"I've been experimenting with recipes from the old days," he said. "Maybe they knew something we forgot."

Dawz sat straighter. "Like what?" The stories from the old days could have some clues about monsters— where they came from and where they liked to hide.

"I don't know. I'll tell you when I figure it out." Dr. Lin's eyes crinkled above the mask. A cautious look, not friendly.

Dawz hopped up as soon as Dr. Lin left him alone, feeling worse than ever. Outside the window, clouds were gathering, and he felt like they were gathering inside too. He paced the room, wishing he could talk to Atlas, wishing his only care was still about how to win the Bakers' Brawl.

Dr. Lin had left the door open a crack, and he could hear Officer Rashmi talking with Pop. He didn't want to speak to either one of them right now, but he couldn't help listening.

". . . and he said the scales Dawz found don't seem

toxic," Officer Rashmi was saying, "but the test in the city will confirm it."

"That's good news." Pop sounded as tired as Dawz felt. Maybe more.

"Sure is. How's Dawz?"

Dawz stiffened. He didn't like to hear them talking about him.

Pop sighed. "I'm worried. Those scales we found make it very real."

"Uh-huh. Do you think we should tell him what happened to Faye?"

A hollow feeling filled Dawz's chest. *Mom?* He crept closer. Close enough to see Pop through the crack. *What about her?*

"I already did." Pop ran his hands through his hair. "Well, I said enough to warn him."

What does that mean? Dawz edged close enough to see them both.

"What did you say?" Officer Rashmi leveled a gaze at Pop. "Not about—"

"No! He thinks Faye was just *hunting* monsters."

The cut on Dawz's cheek pulsed. *If she wasn't hunting monsters, what was she doing?*

"Right. Good." Officer Rashmi nodded. "Because we have no physical proof she turned into one."

A chill rattled through Dawz.

"I know." Pop sounded miserable.

"The witness seemed reliable, but yellow feathers and scorpion tail? It's so . . ."

Silence hung between them, but, for Dawz, it was as loud as a thunderstorm. She'd turned into the same monster she used to talk about? How?

109

"I can't think about Faye that way," Pop said. "I knew she had challenges. Remember I told you she was an anxious kid, always worrying she wasn't safe? I never thought it might be true."

"And now?"

"And now I worry about monsters every day." Pop's voice had a haunted tone. "I worry about what might happen to Dawz."

Dawz stepped away from the doorway, tripping over his own backpack. He was like Mom. And she was a monster. Is that how Pop saw him—as a monster to worry about?

No wonder Pop wanted the tests.

Dr. Lin returned with a clear bottle full of yellow pills and a large jar of cream, and Pop followed him into the room. Dawz barely listened as Dr. Lin ordered him to stay out of school until his cheek healed, even though everyone knew it wasn't going to heal anytime soon, because Thea was getting worse instead of better.

Pop nodded at everything Dr. Lin said, not looking at Dawz, as if he didn't want to see him. If Dawz turned into a monster, what would Pop and Officer Rashmi do to him? Dawz shuddered as he imagined the whole town hunting him. Did the monster feel hunted? Did it even have feelings?

Then Pop's hand was a heavy weight on his shoulder. "Are you listening, Dawz? Dr. Lin says you need to stay home from school until you heal."

If he healed. Dawz shook Pop off. "What about the Bakers' Brawl? Can I go to that?" He knew he shouldn't be talking back, but he didn't care. The Brawl was the only normal thing he had left.

Pop's gaze flickered to Dawz, then away.

"We'll see." Dr. Lin wrinkled his forehead. "With this monster around, they may even cancel it."

Shadows swirled around Dawz, twisting closer.

Chapter 18

Mim ran in a straight line away from Dawz the Horrible. Panting. Straining. Clutching her book and food sack.

Her hearts beat strangely off-tempo. Her too-big insides howled to be fed. Her too-long legs had an awkward gait. Her hooves landed harder, sooner, than they should.

A pole appeared. She darted around it. Then a building. And another. She gave humans a wide berth, always returning to her course. Away from Dawz the Horrible. Far, far away.

Fat tears blurred her vision. She hadn't grown because of the extra space in her closet. No nest, no matter how snug, could halt her growth. She'd grown because of Dawz the Horrible.

If only she could outrun her ghastly large snout and horns and chest and tail. If only she could get far enough away from him that she'd stop growing—maybe she'd even shrink back to normal.

It had to happen.

But first, Mim had to eat. She couldn't resist it. She didn't want food to make her grow even bigger, but her hunger had become too fierce to ignore.

She tore at the larger boy's food sack and pulled out a thing wrapped in paper. Dare she eat it? Would it hurt her?

Her insides roared to be filled.

As she jogged, she bit into the thing, paper and all. She tasted a bready something with spicy meat in the middle, which was better than the lace-up shoe she'd once eaten. She gulped the rest of it down, then licked her fingers.

Feed me, her insides called, as if she'd eaten nothing.

Mim tugged a metal can out of the sack and tried to eat it, but her flat teeth couldn't bite through. Eventually, she punctured it and slurped down the syrupy liquid inside, tossing aside the can because it was too tough to chew. Soon, she could feel the bready something and liquid jostling inside her as she ran, yet her insides still felt empty. Was she eating the wrong things?

She couldn't stop to figure it out. She needed to get away more than she needed to solve this puzzle.

Mim dropped the empty food sack and hurried on. Her hunger chased her. She was grateful when the buildings became few, and the humans too, while the trees became many. Skinny trunks stretching toward the sun. Silly trees that didn't know shade was better.

Crunchy leaves softened the clomp of her hooves. Tree shadows soothed her eyes. The air smelled fresher than any nest she'd known. But Mim couldn't trust it.

She'd followed her snout to her cupboard nest and her garden nest, but Dawz the Horrible had lurked near each one. Why had her own snout deceived her?

Her own snout!

Trust led to him. He led to growing. And growing led to hunger. So she couldn't trust herself. She couldn't trust her too-big everything.

She could have no nest for comfort. No closet, cupboard, or friend with a soothing scent.

No comforts except for her book. Mim held it to her chest as she ran, careful of her new nail-claws—half as long as each finger now, awkward and pointed.

A tear dripped off her snout and onto the book. She wiped it dry with the side of her hand.

She'd won her book back, and she would keep it. Not even Dawz the Horrible could wrench it from her.

She pushed between bushes and over logs, hoping she'd stop growing soon. She glanced down at herself to see another layer of scales peeling off, dropping, and leaving a trail.

No, no, no!

Would Dawz the Horrible follow her? Would he collect her scales and keep them in a sock?

Mim wanted to loop back and pick up all her scales. They were hers. She didn't want his stink all over them.

But she couldn't trust her instincts. She had to do the opposite. She had to keep moving away from him.

Mim left her scales behind.

When the forest ended, Mim ran into a marsh. It smelled rotten. It was wide open to the sunlight that hurt her eyes and heated her insides. It was a perfect place for a monster who couldn't trust herself. Who needed to be everything she was not.

Unfamiliar growls and yelps carried over the marsh, but the creatures that made them stayed far out of sight. Cold water and bog plants swamped her legs, and muck tried to trap her hooves. Mim had to veer off course from her steady path away from Dawz the Horrible. As if the marsh was trying to lead her astray or turn her around. Mim refused to let that happen.

She kept moving away from Dawz the Horrible by resisting her instincts, by traveling in the opposite direction to where they told her to go. Blackflies arrived, clustering over her head, biting her snout, and crawling between her scales. Mim swatted a few into her hand and ate them. Her insides still felt empty.

She lapped up the marsh water with her tongue. It tasted like muck and decay, but she swallowed it anyway. Her hunger called, louder than ever.

White-throated birds darted between clumps of grasses, chirping. Mim tried to catch one, but it darted away. It probably wouldn't have filled her up, anyway. She wished she knew what would.

More scales peeled and dropped, but now they sank into the boggy water. Mim hurried on, slower than before but grateful she was no longer leaving a trail. If Dawz the Horrible made it this far, she'd lose him here.

Once the sun had crossed the sky, Mim's legs screamed for a rest. She felt weak all over, but maybe that was normal for a monster who had never run or grown before—a monster who couldn't figure out what to eat.

She sank onto a moss-covered root that bulged above the marsh and set her book in a dry nook. She stroked the fearsome creatures on the cover for comfort, but they just stared back, silent and still. She opened her book to examine the squiggly black marks once again. The sun beamed onto the pages. Blackflies buzzed around her and bit the soft flesh between her scales in a not-helpful way. And the black marks didn't move, didn't speak, didn't release their magic.

She shut the book and stared at her huge hooves, planted in muck. Her too-big hands with too-big nail-claws lay in her lap. Hideous.

If only she could stop herself from growing. If only she could banish her hunger. If only she hadn't touched Dawz the Horrible.

Before that, she hadn't touched many others. Just a spider or two, and a moth. And she'd scratched the large woman and petted Raar-Sparkle. But none of them had been like Dawz the Horrible.

His touch had shocked her, had threatened to explode her, had been full of memory and feeling in the most horrible way.

Mim's left heart hadn't beat the same since. Like he'd damaged it.

Could he do that just by touching her?

Mim felt one side of her chest, then the other. Yes, the left side was beating faster than the right. Pulsing, pulsing, pulsing to its own music. As if two songs were playing inside her at the same time, and they didn't know how to get along.

Mim tapped on the left side of her chest in the rhythm of the right, hoping the left heart would slow down and get back in sync.

It sped along at its own pace.

And what of the memory she'd gained? She abhorred it. Why had Dawz the Horrible shared it with her?

She hated being linked with him. Hated. It.

If the only creature she could connect to was Dawz the Horrible, she was better off alone.

Mim rocked back and forth on the mossy root. She didn't want to admit what the memory meant, but it haunted her anyway. Dawz the Horrible had been dreaming. Mim knew about dreams. They were flashes of not-true that entered her head, although they felt true. Dreams were tricky.

But this dream had been different from one in Mim's head. It had been Dawz the Horrible's dream, but she'd been in it. Cunning boy who'd dreamed Mim into his head!

She could now remember Dawz the Horrible screaming, "Nononononononono!" Pushing her away. Out of his dream. Into his room.

She'd breathed her first breath then. Taken her first step. She hadn't been sure how to walk, where she was, how she was, or why she was. Dawz the Horrible had woken and screamed something new: "Go away, go away!"

And Mim had. She'd scampered to the closet on her newly formed hooves, chased by the screams—his piercing screams—that burrowed into her and made her shiver. That made her need a closet. That made her build a nest.

Mim tucked her book under her arm. She stood on the root in the middle of the marsh. The sun slanted between the grasses.

Dawz the Horrible had the power to create Mim from his dreams. He had the power to make her grow at a single touch.

Mim didn't want to find out what else he could do.

She waded back into the marsh water and pushed on in a straight line, away from the town and away from the boy who'd dreamed her into being.

Chapter 19

All Tuesday, Dawz had stayed home like Dr. Lin had ordered. He'd eaten the meals Pop made for him. He'd applied Dr. Lin's cream and taken pills without complaining. He'd studied his cryptozoology books, remembering how it used to be scary fun to read about cryptids, and he'd wondered why the monster had taken one of those books. Was it looking for other monsters to do terrible deeds with? He'd made a drawing of the monster for Luiza, which wasn't as good as a police sketch, but he expected she'd like it. He'd also watched online videos about sightings of rare creatures until his eyes hurt, but he didn't see any with a scorpion tail. How long before he turned into a monster like his mother?

By Wednesday afternoon, Dawz had become restless. He had to do something. Like talk to Luiza about the monster stories from the old days to figure out what he was facing. And ask Ronny how to trap a monster long enough for someone to collect it.

Dawz shoved his drawing for Luiza into his backpack, along with a bunch of spare bandages. It had taken a while to figure out how to cover the cut on his cheek so it wouldn't ooze through. He didn't want to disgust people. Especially Pop.

Dawz tiptoed past the kitchen, where Pop was working. He hoped that Pop wouldn't notice him slipping out, that he'd assume Dawz was still resting. The delicious scent of brown sugar and molasses filled the front hall, reminding Dawz of the Bakers' Brawl that was supposed to happen in only three days—if they didn't cancel it because of the monster. Could he find it for Ronny and Officer Rashmi before then? He imagined baking a wonderful dish with Atlas at the Bakers' Brawl—something the judges would adore. Tuna-and-brown-sugar biscuits? Mustard-molasses cookies? Not that he would be able to compete with his Cheek of Extreme Grossness.

Nothing felt fair or right or good.

Dawz jammed his feet into his shoes and reached for the front door.

"Why are you wearing your shoes?" Pop stood in the kitchen doorway, holding a spatula.

Dawz squirmed. "I thought I'd go for a bike ride—"

"No. Dr. Lin said—"

"He said no school. He didn't say I was a prisoner."

Pop waggled the spatula. "You know I don't want you out there alone. It's not—"

"Safe. I know. But I can't stay inside forever."

Pop shook his head. "You know that—"

"I promise not to go near the school. And I'll keep my cut bandaged. I just need . . . I need . . ."

"To stay home."

A fizz of anger bubbled through Dawz like a soda can ready to explode. Was Pop so disgusted by what Dawz might become that he wanted to hide him away? Why had he even adopted Dawz? "Maybe I should stay in my room for the rest of my life!"

"I know this is hard—"

"You don't know anything!" Dawz was yelling now.

A wrinkle formed between Pop's eyebrows as a timer went off in the kitchen. "Maybe I can drive you to Atlas's later, or he could come here."

"Whatever." Dawz stomped up the stairs, already planning how he could sneak out without getting caught. He had no time to waste. What if the monster had already hurt more people?

Dawz waited an hour before his next attempt. He checked his bandages. He threw his shoes and backpack out his bedroom window. He went down to the basement and left the TV on loud. Then he climbed out the basement window. He only felt guilty for a moment. Wasn't he sneaking out for a good reason? He'd be back before Pop noticed he was gone.

Atlas would be in school, so Dawz was on his own. He hadn't seen his friend for two days—since the monster had terrorized the schoolyard—and he missed him more than ever. He sneaked his bike from the shed and aimed it toward Four Corners and the bench where he hoped Luiza would be sitting.

He hadn't felt the prickle at the edge of his left eye since the schoolyard, but he scanned for the monster as he biked. His cheek ached still, and he hated how bulky the bandages were. As he headed toward Four Corners, a mom pulled her kid closer. A bluster of tourists gaped at his bandages. Three patrol cars passed—far more than usual. He tried to stay out of their way in case Officer Rashmi was in one. For sure, she'd report his location to Pop.

As he neared Four Corners, he saw Luiza's bench empty. He slowed his bike and whacked the handlebars like they were to blame.

What now?

He stopped next to her bench. It was close to the Bear Beast statue, with a view of the park and the community center where the Junior Bakers' Brawl teams created their masterpieces. The park workers hadn't even set up the stage where the contest winners were announced, although piles of wood and metal struts lay on the grass. Dawz had stood with Atlas on the stage two times while the Sudbury girls had taken the trophy. How could he get a chance to prove himself if he wasn't allowed to compete? Dawz wanted Dr. Lin's cream to start working. He wanted the contest to go ahead as planned.

A driver who'd stopped at the light eyed him, and so did a couple on the sidewalk. He dismounted with his back to them. Should he wait for Luiza? He didn't like being so near the Bear Beast. He didn't like being near so many nosy people.

Dawz leaned his bike against the bench and took off his helmet. Maybe Luiza would come soon. Maybe he should try to find Ronny first. He'd taken Ronny's card off Pop's pile of papers in the kitchen. It had an address and a phone number.

The couple began taking pictures with the Bear Beast, posing with smiling faces right under its raised claws. He muttered under his breath, "Stupid tourists."

"Stupid for coming north during blackfly season?"

Dawz spun around to see Luiza with a steaming cup from Thea's Café. Coffee. It smelled sweet, rich, and bitter, like the coffee Pop had taught him to make. Atlas had told him that Thea wasn't back to work yet, and Mandi wasn't scheduled to come home from her tour of duty until July, so Thea had hired someone else to run the café until she could get back to it. Dawz felt guilty about Thea all over again.

"That looks nasty." Luiza studied his bandages before taking a seat on the bench near the Bear Beast.

"It is." He didn't like how she pointed it out, but at least she didn't treat him like an infection to be avoided. "I want to talk to you."

"You already are." She sipped her coffee. "I heard about your run-in with the monster in the schoolyard. You okay?"

He wasn't okay, but he nodded anyway. He knew she'd ask questions until she was satisfied, so he recapped, leaving out the part about the monster growing when he touched it.

"Are you ready to set up that sketch artist now?" she asked him.

"I . . . uh . . . made you a sketch." Dawz sat sideways at the far end of the bench, keeping the Bear Beast in sight, as if it might come to life. He rummaged in his backpack for the drawing. Although he still didn't understand how a sketch could help to find the monster when no one else could see it, he was glad he'd brought her this offering. "Sorry it's a bit crumpled." He handed it over.

"Huh." Luiza examined his sketch, and Dawz could see how inaccurate it was. He was a decent artist, but still. "You say it's about your height?"

"Yes." Dawz flushed. He didn't like being compared to the monster. "At least it was. It could be even bigger now."

"In two days?" Luiza raised her eyebrows.

Oops. He'd forgotten she didn't know how it grew when it touched him.

"Maybe. Who knows what it can do?" he shot back at her a little too forcefully. "Why do you want a sketch of it, anyway?"

"For my collection." She folded the paper. "I can keep it?"

"I guess." He knew Luiza had been researching monsters forever, which is how the town got information for the tourist map of monster sightings. He hoped she wouldn't add his closet to the map. "What do you know about where monsters like to hide?"

She crossed her arms. "Why do you want to know about that?"

Couldn't she just help him? "I'm the only one who can see it, so maybe I can help Ronny—the pest-control guy—and Officer Rashmi catch it."

"That's best left to them, don't you think?"

He bit his cheek, realizing he shouldn't have revealed his plan. He tried another question. "Why are there monsters in this town? In my closet?"

"I suspect there've always been monsters here." Luiza studied him. "There's a story I don't often tell because it can be disturbing." She raised one eyebrow. "But maybe you need to hear it?"

He clenched his jaw. A new story. One that might offer answers and fresh terrors. "Yes." He tried to sound brave. "Please, tell me."

"Okay," she said in her familiar story voice. "They say that, at one point, the early townsfolk built a maze of hedges and wooden slats where the park now stands. That when a monster appeared, they lured it into the maze, trapped it there, and then sent a hero in alone to defeat it."

She gazed intensely at the swaying trees and beds of spring flowers in the park, and Dawz did too, imagining something like the Minotaur myth—the solitary hero entering the maze with their head up and shoulders back even though they were terrified, the monster roaring and raging from within the hedges, a crowd jeering and cheering outside.

Dawz hugged his arms to his chest. "Why did the hero have to defeat it?"

Her eyes drilled into his. "The rumor was that they were meant for each other, bonded somehow. In the end, one had to absorb the other. Only one ever walked out of the maze."

A shiver took over Dawz and didn't let go. Had Mom's monster absorbed her? Could it happen to him? "How did they pick the hero?"

"The monster chose the person."

Dawz didn't want to hear that. Heroes shouldn't be chosen by monsters. "Was the hero the only one who could see it?"

"I . . ." Luiza's tone softened. "The story doesn't say."

Dawz sighed. Of course a story couldn't explain what was happening to him. "Does the story say where the monsters came from?"

"No. It just happens around here sometimes." She paused. "Like now."

Like now. "Ronny said this town is closer to the crust of the spirit world, where different types of creatures can get tangled together on the way into life." It sounded stupid when he said it.

"Could be. Maybe when a spirit gets fed enough, it becomes solid."

"Fed enough what?" He couldn't imagine what a spirit ate.

"Whatever it needs to live in our world. What I wonder is . . . how do we deal with a monster once it appears? This is the first one in my lifetime, and yours."

So she hadn't heard about his mom? "We lock it up where it can't hurt anyone." Dawz watched the flowers bob where the maze had once stood. It was all so impossible. But so was a monster in his closet. "Have you ever heard of a monster with a scorpion's tail? And yellow feathers?"

"Doesn't sound familiar. Why? Do you have something else to tell me?"

He shook his head quickly. If she didn't know about Mom, he wasn't going to explain.

She watched him until he squirmed. "Listen, Dawz, people believe the strangest things, especially when they're scared or upset. I think the stories people share are part truth and part not-truth. The hard part is figuring out which is which."

Chapter 20

Mim lay in a narrow cave, face up and panting. Her limbs were dead weights on the rock beneath her. She didn't know whether it was day or night. She didn't know how long she'd lain there.

She'd continued to run away from Dawz the Horrible, peeling and growing. And she'd continued to try to satisfy her insides—first with a meal of leaves and twigs, later with a gray mouse. But her hunger still raged; the things she ate lumped and jiggled inside her; her body still grew; and her scales still peeled.

Mim had cleared the tricky marsh and entered a forest with ragged mounds of rock that forced her to climb over them. She had run from more mysterious growls and yelps, avoiding whatever creatures might be lurking nearby. She had run until she couldn't anymore, until she had to walk, and finally crawl. Until she couldn't lift one hand in front of the other.

Now she was weaker than weak. Her left heart beat even faster, and her right one had slowed to a faint pulse. Mim squeezed her eyes shut and tried to catch her breath. Could this be dying? Like when a spider in her closet nest stopped weaving webs, stopped catching prey, and just sat still until it turned brittle and broke apart?

This couldn't be happening. Not to her.

She had to get up. She had to try harder. Mim forced herself to her hands and knees. She dragged herself out of the cave, pulling her book with her.

Thankfully, it was cloudy outside. She liked how the clouds hung low enough to touch the treetops and settle in hollows. It made the sky seem less colossal.

Mim struggled to her hooves, wobbling. She aimed away from Dawz the Horrible along the same route she'd been traveling. It had become easier to sense where to go by resisting what her instincts told her to do, yet it felt harder to take each step.

Why was she so weak?

Mim sank to her knees and held her snout in her hands. She could hardly think straight, but she forced herself to reason it out. Her hunger was devouring her. It was stealing her strength. She had to figure out what would satisfy her insides. Restore her strength.

But how? She'd tried human food and drink. She'd tried things she'd found in the forest and marsh.

Now she was farther from Dawz the Horrible than she'd ever been. She'd eaten more than she ever had, yet she was hungrier than she'd ever been.

If she couldn't run farther away from him, what else could she do?

Mim gulped in a breath as a terrible idea crept into her head.

Maybe she needed to go back to Dawz the Horrible.

Maybe she needed to eat him.

A shudder shook Mim's insides. *Disgusting!* But she also recalled a book she'd heard the grown-up share one night as she listened from her closet nest. The story had been about a giant, which was a kind of monster. He had yelled *fee-fi-fo-fum*, then tried to eat a boy.

Maybe monsters were supposed to eat boys.

Even if they didn't want to.

Mim turned in the direction of Dawz the Horrible. The journey would be impossible, but she would find a way. She managed to take one step. And another.

But as Mim took more steps, a new thought grew. These steps were easier than she'd expected. Her legs felt less strained, even though her hearts were still beating off-time to one another.

Mim hugged her book. *No. It couldn't be true!*

She tested more and more steps.

It couldn't be *easier* to walk toward Dawz the Horrible.

But it was.

Mim walked on, resenting each step. She wove between evergreens and splashed through a stream. As her hoof slipped on a slimy rock, she slid sideways. Her book dropped into the water.

Mim yelped and dove for it. They both emerged, streaming water.

Mim tried to wring out her book, but it had already swollen.

She rocked her book.

It swelled more.

Mim wailed. It didn't help her book.

Ever since she'd left her closet, everything had gone wrong, and Mim didn't see how it was going to get better.

Not if she needed to find that horrible boy again.

Not if she needed to eat him.

Chapter 21

Dawz didn't mean to stay out so long, but Ronny wasn't an easy guy to track down. The Hug-a-Bug shop was on the far side of town, and Dawz went the wrong way more than once, mostly because Luiza's story had disturbed him. Which parts of it were true? He thought about stories he'd read that felt real. Tales of people who'd been tricked by jinns. The slimy qallupilluit who hid under the Arctic sea ice, luring kids away from their homes. Could a monster absorb a human like Luiza had said? Did the hero really need to battle the monster alone?

He didn't want to find out.

When he finally found the Hug-a-Bug storefront squeezed between an auto shop and the train tracks, a sign taped to the door read *Back in 1 Hour*.

Dawz rattled the door. He paced the parking lot.

No Ronny.

He mounted his bike and clenched his grips. Now

he'd have to try to come back tomorrow. Or maybe he could call Ronny without Pop listening in.

He aimed his bike toward home, hoping Pop hadn't discovered he was gone.

On the way home, Dawz biked by his school. He knew he shouldn't detour, but maybe he'd catch Atlas riding home.

A police car sat out front, and two officers he didn't know were patrolling the yard on foot. Dawz didn't feel the prickle that usually told him the monster was nearby, so he guessed the police were still investigating the last sighting or maybe guarding the school. Caution tape blocked off the garden and the library door. Kids were streaming out the school doors. Dawz cruised to a stop near the corner of the yard—away from the officers and the door where Pop would be picking up Jayla. If he got caught, he'd be in big trouble.

He looked for Atlas by the chain-link fence where they usually locked their bikes.

His bike wasn't there.

Why was no one where they were supposed to be?

Dawz pushed off the curb.

That's when he noticed the Hug-a-Bug van tucked against the side of the building with the back doors open.

Ronny must be here. He was probably investigating the monster sighting too.

Dawz should have thought of that. He'd wasted so much time biking back and forth.

Dawz rode his bike across the grass, even though it wasn't allowed. He had to talk to Ronny, then beat

Pop home. As he neared the van, he could hear Ronny speaking to someone. He'd better not be busy. Dawz had waited long enough. He rounded the corner of the van to see Jayla and Ronny sitting on the bumper. Jayla was swinging her legs and writing in a notebook.

He froze, hoping she wouldn't tell Pop that he'd been here.

"Dawz! Good to see you, lad!" Ronny grinned, although his eyes flickered to the bandages on Dawz's cheek, then away. He was holding a rectangular mesh trap in both hands. Behind him, folded-up traps in different sizes lined the sides of the van.

Dawz straddled his bike. "What are you doing here?" He knew he sounded rude, but he didn't care.

"Your sister and I were talking about how she wants to be a pest controller when she grows up. I was just showing her how this here trap works." Ronny opened and shut the spring-loaded door.

"I've learned lots!" Jayla didn't seem to notice that Dawz was at school when he shouldn't be. "Like how the trap needs to fit the creature. A small trap for a small creature, and a medium trap for a medium creature. I know how to set the latch and where to put the bait."

"You're a fast learner." Ronny smiled.

"Jayla should be waiting where Pop told her to wait." Dawz's temples throbbed. Should he ask her not to tell Pop he was here? Would she listen?

"But I'm doing a school report." Jayla held up her notebook.

Dawz could see a little-kid drawing of a cage trap that had already caught a pretend creature. She'd also drawn a mangled foot caught in a snare trap.

"Did you know you need to remove a creature from a trap as soon as possible?" she said. "And you should never use a snare trap, because they hurt."

Ronny nodded sagely. "Every creature should be treated with care and respect—"

"—no matter how pesky they are to humans," Jayla finished.

Ronny laughed and his belly shook. "And what did you learn about bait, lass?"

It bothered Dawz that Ronny sounded so proud of Jayla. Dawz should be the one learning how to trap a monster. Anyway, monsters shouldn't be cared for like pets.

"The bait needs to match the creature," Jayla said. "A good pest controller asks, 'What kind of bait would lure the creature into the trap?'"

Ronny slapped his knee. "Exactly!"

"Dawz? Jayla!"

Dawz was already cringing when he spun around to see Pop. Pop's hair was out of its ponytail and messed up, and his eyes had a frantic look.

"I didn't mean to—" The words fell out of Dawz's mouth as if they had a life of their own.

"You didn't mean to sneak out?" Pop's voice was pitched high. "Or come to the school when Dr. Lin told you not to? And I hear you were hanging around Four Corners with Luiza!"

Everyone in Morsh was a spy. Pop was frowning at him in that way that usually made Dawz want to make up for it somehow. But today was different. Today, Dawz was tired of Pop's judgmental looks. He didn't understand how monstrous Dawz felt. How hard he was trying to fix this mess.

"And you," Pop said to Jayla. "I said we'd drive to Ronny's shop so you could interview him."

"But I saw his van, and I already had my notebook—"

"We're going home. Now."

Dawz didn't like this new, stricter Pop who treated him like a little kid. He wasn't. What was wrong with getting information from Luiza and Ronny, anyway? Especially when Pop was keeping secrets about Mom.

"Uh, sorry about that." Ronny took off his Hug-a-Bug cap and swiped his forehead with it. "I thought she'd cleared it with you."

"This isn't your fault." Pop put a firm hand on Dawz's shoulder. "Come on. You really need to change those bandages."

Dawz twisted his shoulder free. He'd forgotten about the bandages. He touched them and felt disgusting pus on his fingertips. As he wiped greenish-purple ooze on his jeans, Pop paled.

"I'll meet you at home." Dawz wheeled his bike around. He didn't want to replace his bandages in front of everyone. How many people had seen him like this?

"We'll go together," Pop insisted. "I'll put your bike in the truck."

"Whatever." Dawz pedaled over the grass toward the parking lot, breaking the rule again. But when he neared Pop's pickup truck, he noticed a few kids he knew, and he veered toward home, pedaling hard.

Pop couldn't tell him what to do. He had no clue what Dawz was facing. No one did.

Chapter 22

Dawz pedaled fast so he could beat Pop home. He was sure to get a lecture, so let it happen inside the house, where he'd be confined like a prisoner yet again. But Pop's truck caught up with him sooner than expected, near the house of that bossy older girl from school. He didn't want her to see him with his cheek oozing or hear Pop lecturing him.

He kept pedaling past her house and the next two as well. Jayla waved from the passenger seat of the truck. Pop rolled down her window. "Get in right now," he yelled across her.

"I'll see you at—"

"Now!"

"We're going over to Atlas's place," Jayla said. "I've always wanted to have a playdate there."

"You're kidding." Dawz skidded to a halt next to the sidewalk.

Pop pulled over too. When he got out, his face was

holding back a storm. "I know you're going through a lot, but you need to listen to me. Now, get off your bike so I can put it in the back." Pop gripped Dawz's handlebars.

Dawz wanted to tug his bike free, but he resisted. "Why are we going to Atlas's?" Why was he even allowed to go there?

Pop sighed, and for a moment he looked more tired than angry. "I should be grounding you for running off, but I just got a call for an emergency meeting with the Bakers' Brawl folks over at the community center, and I don't trust you to stay in while I'm out."

Dawz sucked in a breath. "Are they going to cancel?"

Nothing was normal anymore.

Not the Bakers' Brawl and not Pop, who always used to trust him.

Well, Dawz didn't trust Pop anymore either.

Pop's shoulders drooped. "I don't know yet. But maybe it's not the safest time to host out-of-towners. Now, give me your bike."

Dawz's stomach twisted. Townsfolk like them weren't safe either, but he still wanted the Bakers' Brawl to happen. Was that selfish? He got off his bike. "I can put it in."

Pop lifted it easily. "Get in the truck."

Dawz had to sit in the back seat behind Pop, while Jayla smiled from the front.

"We're going to have so much fun at Atlas's place," she said.

Pop handed Dawz some disinfectant wipes and bandages. "Clean yourself up on the way. Thea says you and Jayla can stay there while I'm—"

"I have my own bandages." Dawz took the wipes. "You should take Jayla with you—"

"Hey—" she began.

"—because Atlas and I need to practice our baking in case they don't cancel the contest." It was another lie, since Dawz planned to talk monsters with Atlas and sort out what he'd learned.

"I can help with that!" Jayla said.

"Enough, Dawz." Pop glared at him in the rearview mirror.

"Fine." Dawz sank into his seat. He was going to have trouble talking to Atlas with Jayla eavesdropping.

As Pop steered the truck away from the curb, Dawz ripped the bandages off his cheek fast, so it would sting less. But it still hurt, and for the first time in ages, he felt a prickle at the edge of his left eye. Could it be? Or was it just the sting from the bandages?

"Wait!" he shouted to Pop, gaping out the window, but he couldn't see the monster anywhere.

"I'm late already." Pop drove on. The prickle faded.

"Great," Dawz muttered. How was he supposed to help find the monster when Pop refused to listen?

A few minutes later, Pop stopped the truck in the alley behind Atlas's apartment.

"Yay! We're here!" Jayla singsonged. She opened her door and jumped out.

Dawz sank lower as she hurried around the truck. He'd cleaned and rebandaged his cheek, which had made it ache more. "Does she really have to come?"

"Don't start that again." Pop got out, sliding his seat forward so Dawz could too. "And you shouldn't touch any food in their kitchen. Not until you heal."

If he healed. Pop had to know it may never happen.

Jayla appeared at his window. "Hurry up!"

Dawz got out, resisting the urge to yell at them both.

"I'll pick you up as soon as my meeting's over." Pop climbed back in.

"Whatever." Dawz rolled his eyes as he walked away.

Jayla bobbed beside him. "What are we going to bake? I can do the stirring. I'm super fast at it."

"I always stir." If he was stirring, he wasn't touching the food.

"But Pop said you can't—"

"You'll watch," he said.

"I can do more than watch." Jayla bounced on every step on the way up to Atlas's place.

As soon as Atlas opened the door, Jayla rushed inside. "Where's the kitchen?"

Atlas smiled and followed her. He was already wearing his chef's hat, but Dawz had left his at home, and it felt wrong for Atlas to wear one without him. Dawz trailed them, passing the open door to Atlas's room and the ominously closed door to his moms' room.

At the kitchen counter, Jayla inspected the recipe book and ingredients Atlas had set out.

"How are you feeling?" Atlas eyed Dawz's cheek.

"I'm fine," Dawz said, suddenly self-conscious. He touched his bandages to check they weren't oozy, but they were dry. "But Pop said I'm not allowed to touch any food."

"That makes sense." Atlas nodded, and Dawz wished his friend hadn't agreed with Pop. "At school, the janitor disinfected everywhere the monster had been, plus your desk too. And I've seen tourists wearing masks and gloves. Everyone is . . . jumpy."

"You can say that again," Dawz grumbled.

Jayla knocked over a bag of spelt flour, and it spilled over her arm and the counter.

"Oops!" She dusted herself off before bounding to the living room couch, where she leaned over the back and peered out the windows. "Wow! You can see all of Main Street from here!"

"Sorry she's such a pain," Dawz said.

Atlas wiped the flour into the sink. "She's not so bad."

"How's your mom?"

Another smile crept onto Atlas's face, which surprised Dawz. "She's okay, but you can see for yourself." He strode down the hall and swung open the door to his moms' room.

Dawz hesitated. The monster had sliced his cheek a day after it had scratched her, so whatever was happening to her would happen to him soon. Maybe he didn't want to see her. Maybe Atlas's version of *okay* wasn't good enough. But Jayla was already pushing past Dawz, and he didn't want to refuse Atlas.

As he crossed the threshold into Atlas's moms' room, the air felt thinner and the light dimmed because the window faced a brick wall. In the double bed, Thea was sitting up with papers, a cell phone, and an empty plate resting on her blanket. She wore a cheerful yellow robe, and Sparkle lay at her feet, purring loudly.

Thea wasn't wasting away. Or feverish. Or dying. Her eyes were bright and, if anything, she looked healthy again.

"Dawz! Good to see you. That cheek looks sore." She made a *tsk* sound.

"It's fine," he lied, even though it hurt most of the time.

"Well, not to worry." She held out her injured arm for him to see.

Dawz didn't want to look, but he couldn't anyway because Jayla scrambled in front of him.

"Where's your cut?" she said. "I want to see."

Reluctantly, Dawz peered around Jayla's pom-pom ponytails to glimpse Thea's unbandaged arm.

It wasn't seeping greenish-purple pus. Instead, a greenish-purple scab had formed. Was her arm actually healing?

"Dr. Lin says I can get back to work soon, which is great because I'm getting complaints about how Abdul's been running my café." She grinned.

"But how?" Dawz couldn't believe his eyes.

"My arm started healing this morning. The wound on my leg too. In only a few hours, they'd stopped hurting and scabbed over. I suppose the antibiotics have finally kicked in. Or maybe Dr. Lin's cream is working."

"Medicine is cool! Maybe I should become a doctor," Jayla said. "Although . . . a pest controller is still cooler."

Dawz's head reeled. All along, he'd been terrified that the monster's toxin would do something terrible to Thea and to him. But now, they could both heal as if nothing had happened?

It changed everything.

"You should be better in time to compete in the Bakers' Brawl." Atlas was beaming.

"If they don't cancel it," Dawz added. "Pop's at a meeting right now."

"Maybe this will change their minds," Atlas said hopefully.

"We should tell them—" Dawz began.

"I already told your pop," Thea said. "But Atlas wanted to tell you himself."

"Oh." Dawz felt left out. Pop knew and didn't tell him. When did Pop get so good at keeping secrets?

"I know you thought it was your fault my mom got hurt," Atlas began, "but everything's okay now."

"Uh-huh," Dawz replied, even though he felt far from okay.

"Dr. Lin will help you heal too, and soon we can put this monster business behind us," Thea said, as if she still believed she'd been scratched by Sparkle. As if he really might be free of this monster one day.

"I'd still like to find a monster for a pet." Jayla patted Sparkle, who woke up purring.

"Speaking of pets, we've officially adopted Sparkle." Atlas sounded like a proud big brother.

Thea smiled. "Or maybe she adopted us. She's been good company, and she loves sleeping on my bed. Plus, we couldn't leave her on the streets. My guess is that she was exposed to whatever animal scratched you, which is how she infected me. Luckily, she has no symptoms, although the vet has been treating her."

Atlas shot Dawz a look that said *My mom may never understand about monsters*, and Dawz gave a nod back.

"Wow," Dawz managed to say. "This is all so . . ."

"Unbelievable," Atlas finished.

Dawz nodded again. Exactly. It felt like an impossible dream.

Chapter 23

Mim wobbled into town, clutching her book as if it could hold her up. She kept to a ditch beside the street, wading through more muck and cringing when cars roared by, even though the humans still seemed unable to see her.

Her return journey through forest and marsh had been grueling, but mapping her route back to Dawz the Horrible felt too easy. She wished she couldn't sense where he was.

She plodded on, crossing the street to head deeper into town. Each step brought her closer to where she didn't want to go. Closer to eating what she never wanted to eat.

Her hearts continued to ping off-beat to one another, but the right one now thudded a little faster and the left one had become less frantic. Her hunger still raged, but it was fading as she neared Dawz the

Horrible. As if he could fuel her just by being close. The idea disgusted her, but maybe it meant she didn't need to eat him. Just stay close to him. Forever.

The thought made her scales curl. Why was *he* her fuel? Was there nothing else that could satisfy her insides?

She'd eaten so much that her insides sloshed and lurched. But maybe she hadn't eaten enough. Or maybe she hadn't eaten the right things. Maybe there was something in Dawz the Horrible's town that could fuel her. Something besides him.

Mim continued her route toward Dawz the Horrible because she felt stronger with each step. But she also explored new eats. As she skirted buildings and tromped through gardens, she bit into whatever she found. A tire hanging from a rope tied to a tree. A red plastic bucket. She swallowed a bite of each, plus a gray pebble and a red bug with black spots.

Mim's insides got heavier. Her hunger still called out.

Her route led to a green space with no buildings. There, humans roamed between tables that were piled high with rich-scented things.

Here, thought Mim. *Here, I'll be able to find my fuel.*

Mim crouched and crawled under and between the tables, scurrying around human legs when they got too close. The humans didn't seem to notice her although they sometimes glanced twice at her book tucked under her arm. Each time that happened, Mim hurried on, hiding under a table or behind a bush till the humans moved away.

At one table, Mim grabbed green leafy stuff, swallowed a crunchy bite, and tossed it aside. It tasted better than the tire or bucket but not by much. *Something else?*

"You have the best tomatoes at the farmers' market," one human said to another. "How much for a large box?"

Mim speared one of the things called tomatoes with a nail-claw and popped it into her mouth. Sweetness exploded as she chewed. She ate another and another. If anything could fuel her, she hoped it would be tomatoes.

Mim took a bite of anything that was close enough to grab. She even bit a hat she found on the ground, which wasn't as tasty as the tomatoes.

Soon, Mim's insides began to growl. They began to whine. They grumbled and ached. Mim crawled between some bushes, curled into a ball, and hugged her book against the ache. She rocked back and forth, watching the legs of humans move past her. Her insides rocked too.

Then they grumbled bigger. And bigger. They grumbled so much that the things Mim had eaten burst up from her insides and out of her mouth, narrowly missing her precious book and tumbling onto the dirt under the bushes.

Mim wiped her mouth with the back of her hand and gaped at what had come out of her. Pieces of tire and bucket. The pebble. Stinky marsh water. Chewed tomatoes. Even the bite of lace-up shoe she'd eaten long ago. She could see marks from her teeth on it.

Mim hugged her middle. Her insides had spoken. They'd rejected all she'd eaten. Now they felt empty. And they *still* asked to be filled.

Mim had no choice. She had to get closer to Dawz the Horrible. Perhaps she could rest near him, gathering strength from him until she grew powerful enough to tame him somehow.

She shuddered at the thought of touching him again. But when she got her strength back, she might have to.

Mim picked up her book. The fearsome creatures on the cover and inside the book felt like her only friends. They'd traveled so far with her—from nest to nest—never abandoning her. Mim crawled out from between the bushes. She wobbled away from the scented things and the gathered humans, using her instincts to turn toward Dawz the Horrible. He was even farther into town. She resumed her steady, tired gait toward him.

Soon, she recognized the building where her garden nest had been, and Dawz the Horrible's scent invaded her nostrils.

So close! But where?

Mim trundled on, following his scent through several yards with gardens. Then, for a terrifying moment, she glimpsed the horrible boy beyond a fence. She glared as he stood beside a truck, talking to his grown-up. Those skinny arms and legs. How could this boy hold such power? Her left heart tugged toward him, wanting more fuel. She had to get closer.

But Dawz the Horrible got into the truck with his grown-up, and it sped off before Mim could get to him.

That boy! So tricky.

Mim followed the truck and the scent of Dawz the Horrible, keeping a tight hold on her book. She wished his smell didn't feel like home in the most twisted way.

Eventually, she came to the not-wide street and the large metal bin where she'd first met Raar-Sparkle.

Was Dawz the Horrible at her cupboard nest? He'd better not hurt her friend. Even though Mim was exhausted, and even though Raar-Sparkle had rumbled with Dawz the Horrible, Mim would fight him for her friend.

The stink of Dawz the Horrible grew more intense. She followed it to a tall staircase. It was in the same building as her cupboard nest, but above it.

Mim leaned against the railing to catch her breath, wishing the stairs weren't so high. She climbed one step. And the next. Each step closer to Dawz the Horrible. Each step fueled by his terrible, unexplainable power.

Chapter 24

Dawz checked his bandage in Atlas's bathroom before they started baking. By the time he was done, Jayla was sitting on the kitchen counter discussing toppings for the Pizza of Extreme Greatness.

"How about peppermint and pepper?" She swung her legs, banging her heels into the drawers on each swing. "It's fun to say." She picked up a bunch of peppermint leaves and a shaker of pepper and chanted, "Peppermint and pepper, peppermint and pepper."

"Interesting idea. Or maybe peppermint and hot peppers?" Atlas said, adjusting his chef's hat.

"That's not as fun to say."

"We don't pick ingredients by what's fun to say." Dawz joined them. "And you better get off the counter." Pop never let her do that at home. *Unsanitary*, he said. Like Dawz's cheek.

Would it really heal? Oh, he wanted it to.

"Hi, Dawz." Jayla waved at him without moving off

the counter. "Atlas said I could stir the flour and yeast together."

"That's my job." Dawz knew he sounded like a little kid, and it made him even angrier.

"But Pop said—"

"Pop's not here, is he?"

"We're not stirring anything yet." Atlas glanced between them like he was trying to figure out how to make them get along.

"Yeah, we're not." Dawz tried to make his voice calmer. "Why don't you read to Thea? Didn't you bring a book—"

"I could read her my school report about how to catch a monster!" Jayla's eyes lit up. "It's in my bag. I wrote lots about traps, and I started writing about how to spot a monster."

"She'd like that." Atlas sounded relieved.

When Jayla had disappeared into the bedroom, Dawz muttered, "I thought she'd never leave."

"I don't mind her," Atlas said. "What do you think of peppermint leaves and hot peppers on the pizza?"

Dawz didn't want to admit it was a good idea. He didn't want Jayla to help them create a new recipe. "Whatever. Let's make the dough."

"Sure, but"—he paused—"you can read the instructions. I'll do the rest. Okay?"

Even Atlas made him feel monstrous. He probably didn't even want to do their special handshake because that would mean touching Dawz.

"If you want." Dawz flipped open Atlas's recipe book. It was a thick hardcover with hundreds of recipes—a birthday gift from Dawz that he'd carefully picked out with Pop. They'd spent hours browsing online until they'd found the right one for Atlas—for a friend who no longer wanted to bake with him. Dawz pushed his hurt feelings away and turned to the section on pizza crust.

As he read out the instructions, Atlas measured the yeast, spelt flour, and warm water. Slowly, Dawz shared everything he'd learned from Luiza and Ronny, answering all of Atlas's questions. "I'm the only one who can see the monster, or tell where it is, so I need to *do* something—maybe catch it. But I don't want to touch it in case I make it grow again."

Atlas nodded like it made sense. "I'll help." He plunged his fingers into the sticky dough and began to knead.

"Thanks." Even though Atlas wouldn't let him bake, it was good to be with his friend.

The dough stretched and mixed under Atlas's hands. As Atlas chopped the peppermint leaves and hot peppers, the kitchen began to smell great, and Dawz could almost forget about the monster and what he needed to do.

Almost.

"How will you catch it without touching it?" Atlas said.

"Ronny says I need bait. Something the monster wants. Then I'll set up a trap around the bait."

"What does it want?"

"I'm not sure yet. . . ." Dawz said, although he had an idea. An idea he didn't want to admit.

Sparkle began to meow and pace by the screen door, just as the niggling prickle at the edge of Dawz's left eye made him suddenly alert. *Oh no!* He glanced around. *Where is it?*

"What kind of sauce would be best?" Atlas held up two plump tomatoes. "The usual, or—"

"It's here," Dawz hissed. "The monster."

Atlas dropped the tomatoes. "Where?"

"Come here, kitty. Come here." Jayla had emerged from the bedroom and was trying to pet Sparkle, who was clawing at the screen door now. "Atlas," Jayla called. "I think she wants out. Can I let her out?"

"Only on a leash," Thea said from her room. "It's on a hook by the door. I don't want her wandering loose. Who knows what she might catch?"

Dawz forgot how to breathe. He wasn't ready. He had no net or trap or cage. But he suspected he already had the bait.

Him.

That's why the monster was always showing up wherever he went.

He grabbed Atlas's baking book from the counter and held it like a weapon. Atlas picked up the rolling pin. They stood with their backs to the counter. Maybe Dawz would eventually need to battle this monster alone, like in Luiza's story, but for now he was glad to have Atlas with him.

"Tell me where to aim." Atlas waved the rolling pin like a sword.

"I can't see it yet!" Dawz said, but he knew he would soon. The prickle was growing stronger.

His left eye began to twitch. Then Jayla was running toward them.

"Yes, come here," he yelled. "Get behind us."

"I need this!" Jayla shrieked. She grabbed the bag of spelt flour and raced toward the screen door.

"Don't!" Dawz yelled. This was not the time to bake.

"I think I found the monster!"

"Where?" Fear froze Dawz in place, but he couldn't let the monster get Jayla. He raced after her. Atlas was right behind him.

"Outside!"

"What is going on out there?" Thea called.

Dawz didn't want Jayla to be able to see the monster. He didn't want her to be like him.

"Call the police!" Atlas yelled to Thea.

"Call Ronny!" Jayla and Dawz said at once.

Dawz skidded to a stop behind Jayla. Through the screen door, he could see the monster, hunched on the landing at the top of the stairs, leaning against the railing and panting heavily. A thin trail of smoke wafted from its nostrils. It was massive now—even bigger than he was.

How had it grown more? Could nothing stop it?

"How can you see it?" he asked.

"I spotted the clues. Look!" She pointed. "She has muddy hooves!"

Not a she, Dawz thought, but he didn't argue this time. After all, he didn't really know, did he?

"And she's holding a book." Jayla shoved the cat away from the door with her socked foot. "Move, Sparkle!"

"Don't open the door!" Dawz yelled as Jayla reached for the handle.

Jayla yanked the door open and threw out the bag of flour.

Dawz gasped. The door swung shut. The flour hit the monster on the snout. It spilled open and covered most of it from horn to hoof, dusting it like a first snow. As the rest of the flour coated the landing and the railing, Dawz couldn't help but be impressed by Jayla's quick thinking. Everyone could see the shape of the monster now.

"What are you kids up to?" Thea squeezed into the hallway behind Atlas.

"I see it!" Atlas shoved next to Dawz as they all peered through the screen door. "The flour—"

"And mud on her hooves!" Jayla's face was lit up like it was her birthday.

"Monster?!" Thea towered over them. "A real monster?! But . . . how? But . . . you were right? Oh my! Back up, kids! Now!"

"We told you!" Atlas shot her a satisfied look.

"You did! But I never . . ." Thea shook her head, her mouth flapping. "I should have listened . . ."

Dawz ignored her. The monster shook the bag off its snout and wiped its eyes. It didn't stand up and roar. It didn't swipe through the screen with its toxic claws, which had grown into small daggers that scared Dawz more than anything else. Instead, it wailed.

"It looks hurt." Atlas lowered his rolling pin.

"It looks deadly." Dawz pushed past Jayla, even though every muscle in his body begged him not to. He was worried that he might make the monster grow, but he couldn't let anyone else do what he needed to do.

"Pass the leash," he told Atlas as he opened the door. "We need to trap it. Can you make a slipknot?" They'd learned about knots in one of their cryptozoology books.

"Slipknots are cruel!" Jayla said. "Ronny told me."

"Don't you dare go out there, Dawson Trumble!" Thea reached for him.

Atlas stepped in front of her. "Just don't let it touch you," he warned Dawz.

"Never again." Dawz raised the recipe book high.

Chapter 25

Mim lay panting in the blinding sunlight at the top of the stairs. Dust coated her fur and scales. It blocked her nostrils and gummed her eyes. But she could still see Dawz the Horrible with a book raised over his head like he was going to hit her. Still see the others behind him, staring in a new way that made her feel exposed.

Then Dawz the Horrible swung the book toward her in a fierce way. Mim cowered against the metal railing, gripping her own book to protect it. But before his book could land, the girl grabbed his arm.

"Don't hit her!" she yelled. "Read to her!"

"That's stupid." Dawz the Horrible yanked his arm free.

Behind them, the larger boy was blocking the woman with the moldy smell—the one Mim had scratched—which was fine with her. They should all stay back. Far back.

"Reading will work on her," insisted the girl. "Why else would she be carrying a book?"

"How should I know?" Dawz the Horrible glanced from his book to Mim's.

She held her book tighter. What did *read* mean? Would it hurt?

His book looked solid. It would not be her friend.

Mim warned him off with a snarl that spewed smoke from deep inside her. She felt the urge to tear at him with her nail-claws, but the longer she spent near him, the more her right heart strengthened and her left one calmed.

As if it had found its nest.

Then Mim sneezed. Dust, smoke, and snot exploded out, and her eyes shut from the force of it, just for an instant, but it felt like forever. When she opened them, terrified the boy had advanced on her, she discovered he'd lowered his book. He wasn't going to hit her? He had to be planning something worse.

She trembled, hating that she could smell his stink again now that her nostrils were clear.

He opened the book and flipped through it like he didn't even care if the pages ripped. "What should I read?"

"Anything," the larger boy said.

"Just back away now, Dawz!" called the woman. "Please."

Yes. Back away, thought Mim. *Do not read at me. My everything already hurts.*

She wished she didn't need Dawz the Horrible. She

wished she could get her strength in a new way. But she was stuck with him. Stuck.

Dawz the Horrible stared at a page in the book. "Baking with yeast isn't hard." He snarled the words as if each one was filled with venom and aimed at her.

Mim held on to the railing. *Reading This is reading?*

"You can make your own simple pizza crust at home in minutes."

Reading is how you make words come out of a book?

"You don't need fancy ingredients." Dawz the Horrible's voice got louder and louder, harder and harder, meaner and meaner. "Just follow these easy steps."

How wonderful to read! How dreadful to read with Dawz the Horrible.

Only he could make reading feel like all her scales were peeling off.

Mim sneezed more and more, and she smelled more too. Meanwhile, Dawz the Horrible read about this thing called pizza, yelling every word: *Flour. Kneading. Rolling. Cheese. Sauce.*

Mim didn't like his voice. She didn't like the other humans watching her. Still, her everything felt stronger with each passing moment. She panted less. And she wondered what pizza was.

From what she could tell, it was desirable. It could be eaten. And reading about it made her feel better. Now Mim *wanted* pizza. But she didn't dare ask for it. She didn't want to ask this boy for anything. Ever. It was bad enough that she got her strength from him. Sure, she may not have to eat him, but she didn't want to need him either.

"See?" the girl said. "Everyone likes to be read to, especially a monster who carries a book."

The larger boy hushed her. Dawz the Horrible read more. "Bake until the crust is lightly browned, and the cheese is golden and bubbling."

"Raar?" The sound came from inside the building, behind the nasty humans.

Mim sat up. Could it be?

She sniffed the air. *Yes!* Raar-Sparkle wove through the cluster of human legs toward her.

"No, Sparkle!" bellowed the woman.

Raar-Sparkle kept coming.

"Grab her!" the woman cried out.

Mim opened her arms and readied her lap.

If she couldn't have pizza, she could at least have her friend back.

Chapter 26

Dawz reached for Sparkle. Atlas did too. But Sparkle dodged between them both.

As Dawz stared in horror, she left paw prints in the flour that sprinkled the landing. She stepped between the outstretched arms of the monster, tail high. She sat in its lap, right next to the cryptozoology book it had stolen from Dawz's bedroom. A book now covered in flour and swollen, like it had been dropped in the marsh and left to rot. If that's how the monster treated a book, what would it do to poor Sparkle?

Dawz couldn't bear to watch. He couldn't look away.

The monster raised its clawed hands. It lowered them toward Sparkle. Dawz should rescue her. But how?

Then Sparkle cuddled the monster. The monster wrapped its arms around Sparkle. They rocked back and forth.

As if they were friends.
Friends?

Dawz clenched Atlas's recipe book and gaped at the monster and the cat. Sparkle licked the monster's arm. She cleared a patch of flour to reveal an ugly purple scale. She purred loud enough for him to hear.

The monster stroked Sparkle's back.

It petted.

And petted.

"Why is it *petting* Sparkle?" Dawz asked.

"Maybe they're . . . friends?" Atlas said.

Jayla laughed and clapped her hands with a smack that made the monster snarl.

Meanwhile, Sparkle licked more and more, grooming the monster, cleaning off the flour.

"They can't be friends." Dawz slammed the recipe book shut.

The monster snarled louder, puffing out terrible smoke again.

Dawz glared at the monster, and it glared back with its creepy glowing eyes. He didn't move forward. It didn't back off. Sparkle licked the monster's shoulder.

Should he tackle it? Pull Sparkle to safety? But what would happen when he touched it?

A siren pierced the air. *Finally.* It startled the monster and Sparkle too. Two police cars appeared at either end of the alley, flashing red-and-blue lights, racing toward the stairs.

"They're here!" Dawz shouted, suddenly grateful for Officer Rashmi. Maybe he could forgive her secret conversations with Pop one day. At least she understood the danger.

Sparkle leaped out of the monster's lap.

"Come here, Sparkle," Thea cooed.

Sparkle ran past Dawz, between the others, and into Atlas's apartment. Dawz didn't turn around to see where she went. She was inside, and that was all that mattered.

The monster forced itself to its hooves. It held the railing for balance.

Dawz stepped back.

"Get in!" Atlas pulled him inside and shut the screen door and the wooden one too. "The police will take care of things."

Dawz hoped so. But the monster was tricky. He had to be sure. He peered out the high rectangular window in the door and held his breath.

Chapter 27

The wailing sound penetrated Mim's head. Flashing lights hurt her eyes. As the door shut Dawz the Horrible and the others inside, Mim realized the reading had been a trick. A way to distract her so the wailing could sneak up.

Nasty humans! She gripped the railing for support and snorted smoke at the sound.

It kept coming, closer than ever.

Flee. She needed to flee. But she didn't know where to go. And she didn't have the strength to get far. At the bottom of the stairs, humans jumped from their wailing, flashing cars.

She snarled. Their footsteps rang on the steps and sent vibrations up to the landing, making her head swim. More wailing sounded in the distance. Mim felt like the whole town was rising against her.

A pipe on the brick wall reached up to the roof. Mim climbed onto the railing, which wobbled. She gripped her book in her teeth, then jumped for the pipe, barely grasping it, and began to shinny up. Her arms and legs nearly gave out. The pipe threatened to bend under her weight. But she scurried higher and higher, then dove for the roof as the pipe crumpled and swayed loose.

Mim collapsed on the flat gravel roof with her tail between her legs. Beneath her, the humans on the stairs yelled, but she ignored them.

She rolled onto her back in the gravel, rubbing off the dust, although it still clung to patches of her fur and chafed between her scales.

Then she heard Dawz the Horrible's voice from the landing: "It went up! On the roof! I can hear it!"

Meddling boy! Mim stood and hobbled away as fast as she could.

She reached the end of the roof, her book still clenched between her teeth. Then she climbed over the edge to the next roof. And the next. Ahead of her, the last roof ended at a corner of two streets with green trees and grass beyond. In the not-wide street below, she caught Dawz the Horrible's scent as he followed her. She needed him nearby to get all her strength back, but the wailing, flashing cars were following too. Why did he have to bring them?

Mim hurried from roof to roof. Dawz the Horrible ran to keep pace with her, and the wailing kept trailing.

She made it to the green. Down below, so did he.

After her garden nest, she didn't trust flowers, but she hoped a tree would be safe. She just wanted a hidden place—close to him but not too close. Was that so impossible?

Mim dropped onto the nearest tree branch. It dipped dangerously under her weight. She shimmied along it, over the street and into the green. Then she swung to the next tree and the next, until she reached one with thick needles. She sank among the densest branches near the top of the tree, far above the humans' reach.

Was she hidden? She couldn't see Dawz the Horrible anywhere.

Was she still close enough to get strong? Yes, she could smell him nearby.

Mim clutched her book in one hand and let out a long breath. Around her hung sweet-smelling cones. She clung to the tree's trunk, swaying with it.

The boy's scent grew sharper.

She held her book tighter as he pushed between some bushes near the bottom of her tree.

"It's here!" he called. "In one of these trees!"

The wailing sound came closer too.

Chapter 28

Sirens blared through the park as Dawz paced below the evergreen, anxious for Officer Rashmi and Ronny to catch up with him. He couldn't believe he'd tracked the monster to this tree. He peered into the branches. He couldn't see purple scales or gray fur anywhere, but the prickle at the edge of his left eye told him the monster was somewhere up there.

He hoped it didn't drop on him. Those claws made him shiver. And the size of its jaws now. Even though it had petted Sparkle instead of tearing her to pieces, it was still dangerous.

The tree was halfway between the community center and the street corner where the Bear Beast stood. It was in a denser part of the park, surrounded by bushes he'd scratched himself on while trailing the monster. The tree stretched maybe fifty feet into the air, and branches from the nearby trees entwined with

165

it. Obviously, the monster had climbed from tree to tree, so it could escape the same way.

"Hurry," he urged the police. He was the only one standing between the monster and the rest of town.

Thea had told him not to go outside, not to follow the monster, but Dawz hadn't listened. Now he wished Atlas had followed, but Thea had stopped him and Jayla too. Dawz knew he'd get in trouble later, but he didn't care.

Then, finally, several police cars drove right into the park, stopping on the grass between him and the community center. Their headlights brightened the shadows that were already gathering as the sun set, and flashes from the red-and-blue emergency lights spiraled everywhere. Dawz was grateful to see Ronny's Hug-a-Bug van rumbling to a stop near the street.

The drivers parked at random angles, and soon police officers and Ronny were streaming toward him from all directions, hurrying between bushes and cars like mice running in a maze.

Like the maze Luiza had said once stood on this spot. Dawz hugged himself, remembering her story. When the hero and monster battled, only one walked out of the maze. One absorbed the other.

"It's up there!" He pointed as everyone converged on him. He wanted them to catch it and lock it away forever. He wanted to be done with it for good.

"You did well, lad." Ronny's hand on his shoulder was a relief.

Officer Rashmi appeared, shouting at her team to block off the park before making her way to Dawz.

"Tell me everything," she said.

And Dawz did. While officers swarmed around them and lit up the evergreens with flashlights, he explained how the monster had come to Atlas's place, how it had daggers for claws now, how Jayla had thought to throw flour on it, how it liked reading but he couldn't fathom why, how it had petted a cat without hurting it, and how he was the bait—the thing the monster was after—so it was his fault that it was here, hunting people in their town.

"Whoa, slow down," Ronny said. "None of this is your fault."

"That's right." Officer Rashmi nodded, but she seemed distracted. "Where's your father? We need to get you out of here."

"But what are you going to do with it?" Panic rose in Dawz. "How are you going to get it down? What if the flour rubs off? How are you going to see it without me?"

"We'll take care of everything. Trust me." Officer Rashmi called over a nearby officer.

Trust her? He was trying to forgive her whispered conversations with Pop, but he wasn't sure he trusted her again. Police officers were just grown-ups with badges.

"Make sure Dawz gets home," she told the officer, who was even taller than Pop.

The officer put a firm arm around Dawz's shoulder. "Come with me," he said.

"Wait. . . ." Dawz twisted sideways. He wanted to leave, but he really should stay. "You need me!"

The officer ushered him away, between the idle cars, flashing lights, and rushing police officers. Why didn't the grown-ups understand? They couldn't solve every problem themselves.

As they neared the community center, Pop raced around a corner of the building. His hair was messed up, and his eyes reflected the blue-and-red lights.

"What happened?" Pop grabbed Dawz and hugged him too tight.

Dawz's thoughts swam like fish battling upstream, and he remembered the Bakers' Brawl meeting. "It was canceled, wasn't it?" He broke free of Pop, already despairing. Nothing could be normal. Not with the monster around.

Pop nodded. "I'm so sorry."

Dawz's hands became fists. The monster had infected everything.

"You need to leave the area," said the officer.

"We're going." Pop pushed Dawz away from the park, away from the monster.

The prickle at the edge of Dawz's left eye faded with each step, but it wasn't enough. The whole town felt like a maze now. One he couldn't escape.

Chapter 29

Trapped. Mim was trapped.

Trapped in a tree above a web of humans, cars, and lights.

Trapped with only her book for comfort.

Trapped with Dawz the Horrible moving farther and farther away, making her weaker.

Beneath her tree, voices shouted, shrill and piercing. Car fumes rose to tickle her snout. Red, blue, and white lights beamed into her tree, hurting her eyes and blinding her to the humans' tricky plans.

Could they see the dust that still coated her in places? Would they try to attack? Mim hugged the tree trunk—sticky with sap. She felt the tug to follow Dawz the Horrible, who had known how to trail her and bring these troubling humans too. Her left heart tugged especially hard toward him, still thumping faster than the right one, although being near Dawz the Horrible had calmed it somewhat. She was grateful not to have to eat him, but would she ever be free of him?

Mim sniffed for his trail, wondering how she might get past the humans beneath her. Maybe she could drop down on them and fight her way through, but she wasn't sure she could fight off several at once. Maybe she could slip past them. She watched clouds gather and the sun set, like they knew she needed shadows to hide—at least until she got rid of the dust. She kept an eye on the pesky humans, worrying about their plans. And she licked the patches of dust she could reach.

Raar-Sparkle's scratchy tongue would be the perfect help right now, especially with the itchy dust trapped between Mim's scales. The problem with making a friend was that you missed them when they were gone.

Then a beam of light burst through the needles and cones, as dazzling as sunlight and twice as painful. It swept back and forth, edging closer. Mim squinted and scooted around the trunk, but another beam burst through on that side. She snugged her face against the trunk, trembling. Her eyes could only see ghostly images of the lights, like floating purple circles.

Nasty humans! She squeezed her eyes shut, but the purple circles remained.

Mim felt her tree tremble. Her eyes popped open. Were they trying to shake her loose?

She glanced down, shading her eyes with her hands. *A man! A man climbing her needle tree!*

Mim's hearts fluttered. Her tail flapped. He had to be coming for her.

She could see the helmet on his head. His arms reaching and pulling himself up. He strapped himself onto each branch as he climbed. He was steady. Relentless.

Mim gripped her book in her teeth again and scrambled up her tree. She was exhausted and not at full strength, but she had to get away.

Her tree swayed with the man's movement. The lights followed her, one on each side. Her hooves—not meant for climbing—slipped.

Mim fell.

She slid through the branches, squealing. Down toward the man. The needles scratching. The branches clawing.

"It's coming for you!" A woman's voice rose.

"I see that!" the climbing man called.

Mim tumbled.

She lost her sense of up and down. Then her chest thumped onto a thick branch, stopping her fall and knocking the breath out of her. Her book slipped from her teeth, but she grabbed it in one hand.

The world spun. Within it, she could see the face of the man tilted toward her.

"Well, aren't you something." He aimed a stick at her. "I sure wish I could get a better look at you. The flour helps though."

Mim panted and clung to the branch, desperate for the spinning to stop. She did not like sticks. She did not like them aimed at her.

The beams of light found her.

"Ten feet above you now," yelled the woman. "Do you have a shot?"

"Now, this will hurt a bit," the man said to Mim. "And it'll make you sleepy."

Mim felt a rush of fear. She knew it would hurt a lot. She knew she needed to flee.

She crouched on the branch—book in her teeth again—and leaped.

She wasn't sure which way she'd jumped. It may have been up. It may have been sideways. But it was away from the man.

She streaked through a beam of light, hands out, ready for impact.

Thud. She hit a branch with leaves, not needles. Her hooves scrabbled for a hold. She grabbed with one hand, sliding down until she found her grip.

Now she knew which way was down. And down was where the circle of humans waited. Mim climbed up.

"It jumped!" shouted the man. "I've never seen such a jump!"

"Where is it?" The woman's voice was fainter. Farther away.

"To the left!" A pause. "No, to my left!"

Mim was sore and panting as she clenched her book in her teeth. The beams were still sweeping the needle tree, back and forth, and that kept her climbing up her leafy tree, slow and steady.

Then she climbed sideways—to the next tree and the next. When she reached the highest high of the tallest tree, she sat among the thinnest branches that could hold her and hugged her book.

Raindrops began to fall on her horns and snout. Small at first. Then bigger. They wet her book, and she tried to protect it with her body. They speckled the beams of light that were still sweeping the trees for her.

Then the rain fell harder. It seeped into her fur and trickled between her scales. She felt the last of the dust loosen and wash away.

Good riddance. She used to like the small girl who nested with Dawz the Horrible. She had a fearless way about her that Mim admired. But no more. Not after she threw dust.

But the rain also soaked Mim's book. It sent many of the humans inside their cars, even though they kept the lights beaming, sweeping.

The man climbed down the tree.

Mim watched, tense and panting. Above her, the sky was dark and heavy with clouds. Beneath her, the humans had stopped tromping among the bushes and peering up at her.

She leaped from treetop to treetop, her book in her teeth again, trying not to bend branches or rustle leaves, which were slick with rain now. She knew her book made her visible, but she wasn't willing to leave it behind.

When she was far away from the circle of humans, cars, and lights, she lowered herself down a tree. She was at the corner of the green, where two streets met. She sensed for Dawz the Horrible's whereabouts. And she headed toward him.

Her left heart tugged her forward, thumping fast, while the right one remained steady. She crept from shadow to shadow, avoiding the pools of light from the streetlamps.

The rain gradually slowed, then stopped.

Mim shook herself to dry her fur. She shook her book too, but it didn't help much.

Soon, she neared the nest of Dawz the Horrible. She skulked down his street, wishing she was going anywhere else. The familiar scents from bushes and trees reminded her that she'd once been happy. She'd once had a closet nest. She'd once been the right size—with the top of her head the same height as the doorknob. Now she would be almost as tall as the whole door.

Her life had been perfect. Well, almost perfect. She remembered the ache of wanting a friend to share the joy of a book. She remembered how much it hurt to be alone.

Now she was stuck with Dawz the Horrible forever. He was her boy, and she was his monster. Even though he would use a book as a weapon and reading as a trick, she needed him. It was the ugly truth.

Mim climbed a dense needle tree in a yard across the street from Dawz the Horrible's nest. She didn't want to be close enough that he would sense her. She suspected their bond went both ways because he'd been able to find her cupboard nest and her garden nest.

Across the street, the light was on in the high-up room where Dawz the Horrible slept.

Right now, he would be in his bed. Right now, the grown-up and the small girl would be huddled with him, faces aglow in lamplight. Right now, they would be sharing a book. Sharing the stories and creatures that used to tumble into Mim's closet to play. How she missed her story friends! How she wished those jumbies and wendigos could visit her now! How she wished she'd had a chance to try reading with Raar-Sparkle.

Mim sank onto a branch, grateful to finally rest, and studied her book. The cover now had her teeth marks in it, which made it look fiercer, but some of the pages were stuck together with wet dust.

She could hardly see the black marks on the pages, but a nearby streetlight helped. They had smeared together, no longer marching like ants. But, luckily, the pictures of the monsters didn't look too damaged. She turned the pages carefully, hoping the book hadn't lost its magic. She loved that each page showed a different monster on it. The one with spikes was a lovely shade of green. The one with tusks looked like a fearsome fighter. The one with three heads full of pointed teeth had all three mouths open and roaring.

This thing called reading was powerful. Powerful enough to make Mim love these monsters. Powerful enough to make her want pizza. Powerful enough to make her listen to Dawz the Horrible.

Mim's scales tingled as an idea grew inside her. It was a big idea. Bold. Beautiful. Blossoming. Reading might be a powerful weapon against her horrible boy. Powerful enough to control him. To subdue him. To take all the strength she'd ever need from him.

But could she figure out how to read at him?

Mim hugged her book. She still didn't understand the black marks, now smeared, although she could try to read the pictures at him. It could work, couldn't it?

First, she needed to rest in this tree, near enough to gain strength from Dawz the Horrible. Then, when she was ready, she'd read at him—read pictures of monsters, proud and fierce like her.

Yes, yes, yes. Then Dawz the Horrible would cower. He would bend to her will.

He would let her nest nearby without a fuss.

He would let her absorb his strength whenever she needed it.

He would never come at her with a glowing stick or steal her things.

It would be terribly glorious.

Mim collapsed into a lump with her snout against the trunk. Every muscle ached as she fell asleep. But not for long.

As the hours passed, Mim dreamed of this thing called pizza. She dreamed of books. She dreamed of a life where she controlled a horrible boy by reading at him. And she grew stronger. Maybe she even grew strong enough to break free from him forever.

Chapter 30

Dawz woke late on Thursday after a restless night. He'd hardly slept, wondering where the monster might be. What if it broke free from the adults and came for him? He felt a faint prickle that told him the monster might be nearby. But he didn't know if it was just his nerves.

He got up, avoiding the Froot Loops he'd sprinkled on the floor around his bed. It was a poor defense system for someone who was monster bait, but Pop hadn't let him build a bigger trap last night. "Officer Rashmi and Ronny will take care of us," Pop had said.

Dawz had his doubts. Luiza had said the *hero* needed to battle the monster. That they were *alone* in the maze. That they were *meant* for each other. What if all of that was true?

A shiver took hold of Dawz and didn't let go. Officer Rashmi and Ronny might never catch the monster. It might be his monster to defeat alone, just like his mother had been forced to face her monster by herself.

Dawz had to get the latest update on the monster hunt from Pop, but first he peeled off his bandage to check his cheek in his bedroom mirror, hoping it had miraculously healed during the night.

It still oozed disgusting pus.

If only he could be as lucky as Thea.

He rebandaged his cheek, then headed for the kitchen, still in his pajamas. As he passed Jayla's room, he was surprised to see her there, drawing in her notebook.

"Why are you home?"

"School's canceled today, so I'm working on my monster report." She smiled up at him, holding out her notebook. "Do you want to see?"

"After breakfast." If school was canceled, the monster must still be on the loose. Not that Dawz would've been allowed to go to school or anywhere else, especially after he'd disobeyed Pop and Thea.

Jayla's smile drooped, and Dawz felt rotten. She'd been so helpful yesterday. Brave and smart. She wasn't even mad at him, even though he'd been mean to her.

"Listen, you were great with the monster. That flour trick was brilliant. And reading was a good idea too."

Jayla sat taller. "I know lots of stuff about monsters."

"You do. I'll read your report in a minute. Right now I need to check if Officer Rashmi and Ronny have captured the monster. Okay?" Until it was locked up, he was bait in a trap.

"Hurry back," she said. "I'll show you everything."

The kitchen was filled with the scent of Pop's savory bastilla pies—one of the recipes he'd taught Dawz back when life was normal. Rows of mouthwatering pastries sat cooling, while Pop kneaded more dough.

"I'm glad you're up." His gaze landed on Dawz's cheek. "Dr. Lin will be stopping by to check on you soon. How're you feeling?"

"It hasn't started healing yet, if that's what you're asking." He put a hand over his bandage. "Did they catch the monster?"

The creases in Pop's forehead deepened. "We'll hear when they do." He dusted flour off his hands and then pulled a sheet of roasted almonds from the oven, filling the air with a nutty scent. Last time they'd made this recipe, roasting the almonds had been Dawz's job.

"It's been hours." Dawz slumped against the island, where Pop had left out a plate of cranberry muffins with a pot of jam. "Can we call Officer Rashmi or Ronny?"

"They'll call when they have something to tell us."

Dawz thumped a muffin onto his plate. Pop didn't understand. The monster was after Dawz. If Officer Rashmi and Ronny couldn't stop it, he would have to.

He considered calling Ronny or the police station himself. But he hated to admit that Pop was right. Officer Rashmi and Ronny would have told them if they'd caught the monster.

"After you eat, can you check on Jayla?" Pop stirred the pie filling in a pan on the stove. "I'm behind on so many orders."

"I just saw her, and she's fine." He bit into the muffin. Sour with the right amount of sweet. It reminded him of the canceled Bakers' Brawl and how everything good was falling away and soon this monster would be all that was left. Was that what had happened to Mom? Was that why she left to hunt her monster?

"Maybe you could do something with her after Dr. Lin visits?" Pop said.

Dawz wanted to refuse. Why should he be helpful when Pop wasn't? Besides, Jayla didn't need to be watched. If she was smart enough to throw flour on a monster she couldn't see, then she could handle a morning alone in her room.

That's when an idea came to Dawz. Maybe he didn't need to face the monster all by himself. After all, it hadn't worked out for Mom. At least he could get help preparing.

"I'll watch her if Atlas can come over," he said.

"I don't think that's a good idea—"

"I want to build monster traps. Jayla can help." She'd proved how useful she was.

"Why? You're not leaving this house or hunting that monster—"

"They're for around my bed. Because I can't sleep at night." And because he needed to be ready for this monster—day or night.

Pop took off his oven mitts. "You know Officer Rashmi and Ronny are doing all they can to keep us safe in the house, right?"

Dawz leveled a gaze at Pop. Nowhere was safe. "Traps won't hurt. I need to do *something*."

Pop sighed. "Fine. Atlas can come after Dr. Lin's gone. If it's okay with Thea."

Chapter 31

Dawz called Atlas, who convinced Thea to let him come over after lunch. When Dawz told Jayla they were going to build traps with Atlas, she shoved her notebook at him.

"Good thing I invented a trap." She pointed to her drawing of one made from an upside-down umbrella. It was baited with books. "See?"

"That might work, but won't we need something stronger than an umbrella? The monster could tear it apart."

"Exactly." She pointed again. "This trap has a bell. If the monster rips the umbrella, the bell will warn us she's here."

She. Was it a *she*? He tried not to think about it.

"But if she reaches into the trap for the books," Jayla continued, "this knot will hold her arm. It may only trap her long enough to ring the bell, but we'll know where she is. It's a warning trap!"

Wow, he'd underestimated Jayla. "Let's see what else you've got in that monster report."

"I have this idea for a monster bomb." She grinned.

"What?" He sat on the floor beside her. "Show me."

When Dr. Lin arrived, he examined Dawz in the large bathroom off Pop's bedroom while Pop hovered in the doorway. Dr. Lin put on his gloves and mask. He explained that the city lab tests on the monster's scales came back as negative for toxins, although Dawz's tests had shown he had an unidentified infection.

No kidding.

Dr. Lin shone a headlamp on him and leaned in close, his stale coffee breath escaping from his mask. When Dr. Lin peeled off Dawz's bandage with his gloved hand, his eyebrows rose.

How bad was it?

"Just as I suspected." Dr. Lin switched off his headlamp and took off his gloves and mask. As if Dawz wasn't toxic anymore.

"It's better?" Dawz dared to hope. "Like Thea's cuts?" Maybe Dr. Lin's cream had worked. Or the medicine. Maybe this proved that Dawz didn't have to handle everything by himself.

"See for yourself." Dr. Lin smiled and stepped back so Dawz could see in the mirror over the sink. "The infection has cleared. I'll monitor it, but you've turned a corner."

Dawz gazed at his reflection, touching the rough patch of skin on his cheek. It was no longer oozing. It had a greenish-purple scab, which was bad enough, but not as bad. "Can I go out now? Can I bake?"

"Wait one more day. But then, yes, you can."

Finally some good news. "Isn't that great, Pop?" Dawz turned to where Pop was leaning against the doorframe, his eyebrows knotted like pretzels as he typed on his phone.

"Pop?" Dawz's voice came out high-pitched. What could be more important than this?

"That's excellent news," Pop said, but he didn't sound convinced.

The words pricked at Dawz.

Maybe Pop would never stop worrying that Dawz would become a monster like Mom.

It was great to be rid of the pus, but Dawz wanted the greenish-purple scab to fade as soon as possible. For the rest of the morning, he kept ducking into Pop's bathroom to see if it had healed yet. Before lunch, Dawz dug out Pop's handheld mirror—the one that could magnify his cheek.

That's when Dawz saw them.

Tiny scales. In. His. Scab.

Where the green had faded.

Purple scales so small he couldn't see them without the magnification.

Scales! On *his* cheek.

He scrubbed at them with soap and a cloth, then examined his cheek in the mirror again. The green had flaked off to reveal more scales.

Dawz's hands began to tremble.

He wasn't healing. He was becoming a monster. Maybe this was how the monster would absorb him. By infecting him, then taking him over, scale by scale.

It was a secret too terrifying to share. Not with Pop. Not with Jayla. Not even with Atlas.

He wished he could run away from it. Banish it before anyone found out.

Had Thea developed scales? But Atlas would've told Dawz if that happened.

Dawz's fingers fumbled as he covered his scales with three bandages. He was the most monstrous human in the whole world.

Atlas arrived in time to help Dawz and Jayla haul their supplies to the backyard, which Pop had reluctantly agreed to let them use. He was still cooking in the kitchen, and every so often his head would appear at the window to check on them. Dawz could imagine the look on Pop's face when he discovered Dawz's scaly cheek.

"My mom didn't want me to come here." Atlas dropped two jugs of molasses beside the empty water balloons. "Because the monster's always showing up where you are."

"Maybe she's right." Dawz sank onto the picnic-table bench. He couldn't shake the feeling that asking for Atlas's help had been a mistake. Maybe he shouldn't be near anyone he cared about. Maybe he shouldn't be near anyone at all.

"Shut up." Atlas plopped next to him. "I told her that you were my friend, and you needed my help. And I reminded her about the extra patrol cars around your house."

"Extra patrols?"

"Yeah, didn't you know?"

Dawz frowned. "Pop didn't mention them. He just keeps saying that Ronny and Officer Rashmi will keep us safe, but I'm not sure they can. How are your mom's scabs?" He wondered what Atlas would think of his scales if he found out.

"Fine." Atlas didn't seem concerned. "Let's make some monster traps. Then you'll feel better."

"Don't forget about the monster bombs." Jayla appeared around the corner of the house, carrying an overstuffed cardboard box. "They're made of balloons filled with sticky, brown molasses. If the monster shows up, we throw them at her so everyone can see her."

"Cool idea! I'll make those." Atlas sounded cheerful. Too cheerful.

"I'll make the traps." Jayla began unpacking books, netting, rope, bells, and umbrellas, while Atlas opened a jug of molasses. Dawz touched his bandages, confirming they were still in place. Somehow, he needed to fix his cheek before anyone found out. If he destroyed the monster, would it help? Dawz shuddered at the thought. His mom had tried and failed.

"Did you hear me?" Atlas was peering at him. "What's wrong with you?"

Everything, Dawz wanted to say.

Atlas mimed throwing a monster bomb across the yard. "We could mix hot sauce into the molasses so it would sting."

"Sure." Dawz tried to sound positive. "But what if it lands on us?"

"Never thought of that." Atlas looked thoughtful.

"Plus, we don't want to hurt the monster," Jayla said.

Unless I have to. Dawz picked up a jug of molasses.

Somehow, he had to figure out how to get rid of his scales before anyone found out about them—even if that meant battling the monster.

Atlas and Dawz set to work filling the balloons. Dawz snapped the opening of the first balloon over the nozzle of a molasses jug, and Atlas squeezed the jug until the balloon filled. It was a sticky job, and soon their hands were coated in molasses, which made tying the balloons a gooey challenge. But they slowly got better at it. When they ran out of molasses, Pop gave them a few squeeze-bottles of buckwheat honey as a sticky replacement. In an hour, they'd filled their three backpacks with monster bombs.

Atlas finished rinsing his hands under Pop's garden hose. "Now what?"

"We set up the traps!" Jayla beamed. "I made four of them."

Her traps were the upside-down umbrellas filled with three books each. She'd attached a netting over the open side of each umbrella, leaving a narrow gap in the netting for the monster to reach an arm through to get the books. Around the gap, she'd fashioned a knot to hold the monster's arm if it reached for a book. The knot linked to the warning bell that would ring if the trap was sprung or ripped open.

"You and I can hide with bombs to throw—" Atlas said to her, already lifting his backpack.

"And Dawz can read to the monster," Jayla finished. "That will lure her in."

"How will you know when to throw them?" Dawz was already wishing he didn't have to be the bait.

"When she springs one of the warning traps," Jayla said like it was obvious.

"I can't wait to see these traps work!" Atlas pretended to get his arm stuck in one. "I can ask to stay for a sleepover, in case it comes at night."

"I can sleep in Dawz's room too," Jayla suggested.

For once, Dawz didn't mind if Jayla crashed his sleepover with Atlas.

Chapter 32

Late in the afternoon, Dawz stood guard as Jayla and Atlas set up one trap outside by the back door and then another by the front. Officer Rashmi and Ronny should have caught the monster by now, but they obviously hadn't because the prickle at the edge of Dawz's left eye kept coming and going, as if the monster might be circling to taunt him. Out front, he scanned the street with his fists tight.

He almost wanted the monster to attack already. He wanted to be done with it.

He followed Jayla and Atlas inside as they dragged the last two traps to his room, setting them up on either side of his bed. Each trap was tied to something—Dawz's dresser or the latch on one of the windows—so the monster couldn't drag it away after it was caught.

"We should show Ronny what we did." Jayla's eyes sparkled.

"We will—right after we catch the monster." Atlas sounded way too eager.

"Okay." Jayla dropped a book on the bed. "Now, you sit and read," she told Dawz.

He pressed his bandages flat for the millionth time to make sure they were covering his scales, but this time he could feel lumps through the bandages. As if his scales were growing.

His hands shook as he set his backpack of monster bombs next to his pillow. He tried not to think about what he was becoming.

"Let's do this," he said. They just needed to catch the monster somehow. It had started all this, so it could end it too, couldn't it?

Unless the monster ended Dawz first.

He sat on his bed and picked up the book. It was one of his favorite novels—about a girl named Nuzira who defeated an army of giant spiders by tricking them. He was only facing one monster, but it was just as deadly.

"Where will you be?" he asked Jayla and Atlas. They each held a backpack of bombs.

"We'll hide somewhere nearby," Atlas said. "We can bomb the monster when it springs a trap."

"Yes!" Jayla bounced in place. "I can watch the hall from my room."

"And I'll hide in Dawz's closet." Atlas unlocked the door and opened it.

Dawz cringed as his friend willingly went inside. He would never get used to unlocked closets. Never.

The smell of Pop's chicken soup drifted up from the kitchen. Dawz ignored his growling stomach and opened the book to a random page.

"The invading spiders advanced across the field toward her," he read, "but Nuzira refused to run."

He felt foolish reading aloud, and he didn't feel a prickle at the edge of his left eye at the moment, so the monster was probably too far away to hear him.

"She raised her shield and waved her sword over her head. 'We will stand strong,' she called to her troops. They were a ragged bunch, already battle-weary, but they waved their swords and chanted back at her, 'Stand strong!'"

He understood how Nuzira's troops felt. Waiting for something to happen was unnerving. Waiting for something monstrous was worse.

Dawz read about the spiders' hairy legs as tall as tree trunks. Their fangs dripping with venom. He wished he was hiding like Atlas and Jayla. He wished he was brave like Nuzira.

He wished he wasn't growing scales.

Just as Nuzira clashed with the largest spider of all, Dawz heard a creak in the hall. He leaped to his feet, ready to hurl the book at whatever might enter. But should he let the traps do their job first? Atlas burst from the closet with a bomb ready to throw. From her room, Jayla yelled something he couldn't hear.

His door swung open. Pop entered with hands above his head. "I surrender!"

Dawz sank onto his bed, his chest hammering.

"So these are the traps?" Pop's smile didn't reach his eyes.

Jayla explained their plans, and Atlas joined in.

"Impressive." Pop examined their backpacks of

bombs. "Hopefully you don't need to throw those inside the house."

Once again, Pop didn't understand. Who cared about a mess when a monster attacked?

"Have Ronny and Officer Rashmi caught the monster?" Dawz hoped the impossible had happened.

Pop looked uneasy. "They're ... uh ... looking for it."

Dawz felt his face get hot. "I led them right to it."

"It slipped away, but they'll find it again. Try not to worry." Pop's voice was forced. "Now, dinner's ready. Chicken soup, anyone?"

How could he not worry? Dawz's stomach growled, as if all that mattered was food.

Atlas licked his lips. "It smells great. But we'll need to bring our bombs, just in case."

"Should we bring the traps too?" Jayla asked.

"Let's leave them here. We still have the ones in the yard."

"Okay." Jayla crossed the room.

Dawz picked up his backpack. As he hoisted it onto one shoulder, a strap slid against his cheek and caught on a sticky, curled-up edge of a bandage.

He tugged. All his bandages ripped off his cheek at once, stinging his skin before swinging through the air stuck to his strap. His cheek chilled.

Pop gasped. "Dawz! Your face!"

Dawz slapped a hand over his scales. How much had they seen?

"He's gone scaly!" Jayla gaped. "And purple?"

Atlas only grunted, and for once Dawz couldn't tell what it meant. But his friend's stare was enough to make him hang his head.

Now everyone knew. He was part monster. Hideous. He couldn't hide it anymore.

A terrible pause filled his room.

He disgusted them. He knew it. He disgusted himself.

Pop took out his phone and started pressing buttons. "I'll call Dr. Lin. Atlas, your mom should pick you up. Dr. Lin should check her too."

Atlas's eyes bulged. "Do you think she's growing scales too?"

Dawz felt even more monstrous. If she was, he was to blame.

"Can I touch them?" Jayla inched closer, raising a hand to his cheek.

"Don't!" He retreated to his bed, but Pop had already yanked her back in a way that curdled Dawz's insides.

"Jayla, go to your room! Atlas, use the kitchen phone to check on your mom. Dawz, don't . . . don't do anything!"

Pop was talking into his phone, explaining what had happened to Dr. Lin while propelling Jayla and Atlas out of the room, and Dawz was wishing he could escape himself.

He hurried to the mirror above his dresser, even though Pop had told him not to move.

His scales were thicker. More defined. Creeping toward his left eye like a sickness.

He sank to the floor.

Pop was right to get everyone away from him.

Soon, the scales would take over. Soon, he wouldn't be a boy anymore. Soon, the monster would consume him, just like in Luiza's story.

Pop burst back into the room, knocking the door wide open, his long hair flying behind him. "Okay, Thea is on her way here. She noticed some scaling in her scabs, but we don't need to panic yet. Dr. Lin will come here too and check you both out." He stared at Dawz. "Why are you on the floor?"

"Not her too." Dawz moaned, hunching over to hide his face. Everything was so wrong. He didn't even feel like the same species as Pop and Jayla, and maybe Thea wasn't anymore either.

Dawz couldn't hurt anyone else. He couldn't face Atlas, who surely wouldn't be his friend anymore. Suddenly, Dawz knew why Mom had left. To protect him and Jayla. To hide her shame.

"Pop, I—" Dawz felt the sting of Pop's ice-blue eyes. He shouldn't even call him Pop anymore. He should be banished from his family, his school, his town. He should banish himself. He got to his feet. "I need to go." He covered his cheek with his hand. "I need to stay away from you and—"

"What? No!" Pop grabbed Dawz's hand and lowered it.

"I don't want to infect you." He pulled, but Pop held tight.

"Stop it, Dawz."

"I have to!" Dawz tugged to free himself. He wasn't sure where he'd go—just away. Far away.

Pop grabbed both his shoulders. "Listen to me. I wasn't there when Faye needed me, but I'm here for you."

"You sent Atlas and Jayla away. Like I'm a—"

"So I could focus on you. You're my son, Dawz. I'm not going anywhere, and neither are you. Okay?"

Dawz wanted to believe. He needed to believe. But

was he really Pop's son when he was part monster? "I'm your adopted son, not your real one," he said.

"An adopted son *is* a real son," Pop insisted. "You, me, and Jayla—we're a family. A family who accepts and helps one another, no matter what. Nothing will change that."

"But you told Officer Rashmi that you worried what I might become."

"Of course I worry about you. I worry because I care about you."

"Even if I have scales?"

"Yes." Pop released him. "Even then. Why didn't you tell me about them?"

"I was going to fix it."

"By yourself?"

"I heard you talking to Officer Rashmi. You said Mom became a monster, and I didn't want you to . . ." Dawz couldn't say it. Who could love a monster? He scrubbed his eyes. "You said you were afraid . . ."

"Not of her! Or you! I've always loved you both! Oh, Dawz, I'm sorry you found out about Faye that way." Pop hugged him, pressing Dawz's scaly cheek against his flannel shirt.

Dawz couldn't breathe for a moment. Pop wasn't afraid of him. He didn't hate him.

He wrapped his arms around Pop and hung on, inhaling the chicken-soup smell in the folds of his shirt. Pop had always smelled like home, and Dawz wanted to breathe it in forever. "What happened to Mom?"

Pop sat on the bed and pulled Dawz down beside him. "I suppose you have a right to know. But I'm not exactly sure. I guess that's why I never told you. Officer Rashmi and I . . . we were trying to protect you."

Dawz frowned. "Not knowing is worse."

"I never thought of that." A shadow crossed Pop's face. "Okay then, I know that Officer Rashmi found a witness. A motel owner who'd rented Faye a room. He said Faye was limping and badly scratched."

Dawz felt limp too. He could guess how she got those scratches.

How she got infected.

How she turned into a monster.

"At night, a sound woke the motel owner. He opened his curtains to see a monster coming out of Faye's room. It was wearing Faye's jacket." Pop's voice broke. "It had yellow feathers—"

"And a scorpion tail," Dawz finished.

"How did you—"

"Mom talked about it. Before she . . . left."

Pop raised his eyebrows. "Oh, Dawz. You didn't need to deal with that by yourself." He said it like he meant it. Like he'd help Dawz through anything.

Dawz's hands began to shake. "What happened next?" He needed to hear every awful detail.

Pop's eyes got a distant look. "The monster ran off. The room was sacked. Faye was gone."

Gone. His mother was gone. Perhaps the monster absorbed her. "For good?" Dawz didn't want to admit that he'd wanted her gone. What kind of son felt that way about his own mother?

"I think so." Pop looked defeated. "From now on, no more secrets, okay? You'll tell me everything, and I'll answer all your questions?"

"I guess." Dawz wasn't sure he could tell Pop *everything*. But he could try.

Just then, a faint jingle came from downstairs. Or was it outside?

"I hope that's Dr. Lin at the door." Pop turned to go, just as Dawz felt the prickle at the edge of his left eye.

"It's here!" He gripped his knapsack of bombs. "The monster is here."

Pop paled. "I'll call Officer Rashmi."

Dawz doubted Officer Rashmi could help. He doubted anyone could.

Chapter 33

Mim circled the nest of Dawz the Horrible. Outside, she'd found books—trapped books—in two places. She studied them from a distance and up close, wondering why they were trapped. She suspected they were a trick, but she didn't know what kind.

Now in the front yard, she decided she had to free them. Holding her own book in one hand, she clawed at the netting that held the trapped books. A ringing sound pealed out.

She froze, and the ringing stopped. It reminded her of the piercing sound that woke her from her garden nest, but it was softer. She found the source of it attached to the netting, ripped it off, and flattened it under her hoof.

The ringing had probably warned Dawz the Horrible that she was there, but it was worth it to rescue the books.

She pulled them free and glared at his window on the top floor. Light beamed into the night, and she sensed him up there, waiting for her.

She should be worried about what other tricks he'd planned, but she wasn't. After resting near him, her everything no longer ached, and her strength had doubled with her size. Soon, Dawz the Horrible would tremble. Soon, she would control him with her book.

She set the new books beside the ruined trap. They were hers now, and she'd come back for them. But she held on to her monster book, her weapon. Then she smashed the blinding light above the door, welcoming the shadows that soothed her eyes. She wanted to enter through a high-up window, since that's how she'd left, but it was a long climb up the brick wall with only narrow cracks to grip onto. She tried to lodge a hoof between two of the bricks, but it wouldn't fit.

Mim turned the knob on the door.

The door didn't budge.

No lock would keep her out.

Mim waited until no cars were passing by on the street, then she butted the door with her horns. She could hear shouts from inside, but she kept at it. After only three whacks, the wood splintered. Mim pushed the door open, watchful for traps.

Lights shone in an empty hall, making her squint. The hall had doorways into rooms that were strangely silent. She stepped inside, inhaling a tangle of human scents and trying to focus on Dawz the Horrible's sweet-tangy one, which used to smell like a place to nest but now smelled like a trick.

Mim's tail fluttered. She'd expected him to be ready to attack.

She smashed a light fixed to a wall and another one on a nearby table, partly to announce her arrival and partly to let the shadows invade the house too. Then she edged forward, clutching her book.

The floor creaked as she moved. Her right heart beat calmly, but her left one tugged her farther into the building. Before, she'd sensed her horrible boy up near her closet, but now she could tell he was down near the ground—a good thing because she didn't know how to get to the up.

She stepped into a large room, smelling her way. The room had a couch and several wide chairs, and she identified the scent of the larger boy and the girl who'd thrown dust, just as they exploded out from behind the couch.

"There! A book floating by the broken lamp!" the girl yelled, then she lobbed a ball-shaped something toward Mim.

The larger boy grunted as he threw too.

Mim easily sidestepped the somethings because her stronger hooves had become sure of themselves. The somethings smacked onto the floor where she'd been standing, exploding out to splatter her hooves with a gooey mess that smelled sweet.

"Did we hit her?" the girl asked.

"Dunno!"

Then Dawz the Horrible burst from behind a chair, and her hearts quickened. *Finally.* She stomped toward him as his grown-up appeared there too. The grown-up yelled, and her horrible boy threw a something, so Mim dodged. *Thump.* The something hit her midthigh, then exploded sweet goo over her furry legs.

She snarled until they all backed off, then she sniffed at the sticky goo, but it seemed harmless.

These goo balls couldn't wound her. These humans had no claws, no horns. Nothing could stop her from confronting her horrible boy, who cowered behind a chair.

Nothing.

She barreled toward him as another goo ball hit her back.

"She's moving!" the girl yelled.

"Keep your distance," ordered the grown-up.

Let them throw. Mim dodged most of the mess. She could see her horrible boy's eyes growing wider and wider. Light from the next room shone on his face, and she noticed impressive purple scales that fanned toward his eye. How had he grown them?

He ran, calling, "If you want me, come get me!"

"Dawz, no!" his grown-up cried out. "Stay with us!"

But her horrible boy kept going, and Mim followed. She could hear the others clomping after them both, but she didn't care. What harm could they do?

The building was a maze of hallways and rooms. Mim trailed her horrible boy to a large space full of cupboards that smelled of human food.

He backed against a row of cupboards, trembling nicely. Mim faced him down, curious about those scales on his face, even though she needed to stay focused on her plan. She heard the others thumping closer, then saw them appear in the doorway. She stood sideways, blocking them from her horrible boy with her bulk and watching that they didn't get too close.

"Please, don't do anything dangerous, Dawz!" the grown-up called over Mim.

"I have to," her horrible boy said. "This is my fight."

"This is our fight," the larger boy shot back.

Her horrible boy looked relieved. "Okay, but I just need to . . . I need to ask it . . ." His eyes found Mim's. "Why do I have these scales?"

How would she know? Mim snarled to shut them all up.

The girl threw one goo ball, then another at Mim, who stepped forward to avoid them, keeping her boy barricaded. By now, Mim's back was coated in the sticky stuff, and it had splashed the cover of her book.

"You will listen to me," she tried to tell Dawz the Horrible. With her bigger throat and lungs, her voice came out rougher and louder than she expected.

"What's happening?" the larger boy said. "Did it answer you?"

"Just please keep back, Atlas," the grown-up said. "Officer Rashmi and Ronny will be here any second."

Mim opened her book. Her hands shook, but she told them not to. Monsters didn't shake when they read at their boys.

"Why is it still carrying that book around?" the larger boy said.

"She must really like it," the girl added.

Mim opened her mouth. She hoped the pictures would just beam words into her mouth—especially since she was reading at her own boy, who was her strength and creator. Surely, the monsters in the pictures knew Mim was supposed to read at him, to make him feel her power over him.

Nothing happened.

Had the rain ruined her book? Or the dust? Or the goo? Maybe its magic had leaked out. *Please work, book*, she begged.

"Dawz, what's it doing now?" The larger boy gazed in her direction, and Mim realized that the goo balls had made her partly visible, partly exposed and vulnerable. She snarled and he backed into the grown-up.

"I think it's trying to *read*." Mim's horrible boy stared.

"What? Why?"

"Maybe it's trying to tell me something about these scales?" He sounded hopeful. "How do I get rid of them?" he asked Mim.

Why would he want to? Mim flipped pages in her book, willing it to work. Maybe her plan was a mistake. Maybe she shouldn't have come here.

A terrible thought blossomed in her mind. Since Dawz the Horrible had created her, could he destroy her too?

Mim backed against a cupboard, still flipping pages.

"What's happening now?" the grown-up demanded.

"I think it's . . . scared?" Mim's horrible boy said.

Mim landed on the page with a picture of her

favorite monster. The one with the many mouths, open and roaring.

Roar at them, it told her. *Be a monster.*

Yes! I will. I can. She was a monster, proud, strong, and fierce.

Chapter 34

Mim stood tall, noticing that she was bigger than the grown-up now. If she couldn't make the book beam its words into her mouth, she would roar her own.

She advanced on Dawz the Horrible, stopping a few steps from him, yet still standing sideways so she could keep an eye on the others. "I will read at you now," she roared. Smoke and ash streamed from her snout, and she controlled her voice better this time.

Mim's horrible boy coughed and waved the smoke away from his face, although no one else seemed to notice it wafting through the room.

Just then, Mim heard familiar wailing from outside. She saw red-and-blue flashing lights through a window. *Not again.*

"They're here!" the larger boy said as more grown-ups burst into the room, crowding behind the others.

"Where is it?" a woman shouted, and Mim

recognized her shouting voice from before—when lights had chased her through trees.

"There!" The horrible boy's grown-up pointed in Mim's direction.

"I smell . . . molasses?"

Then Mim saw the man who'd climbed her tree. He was aiming a stick at her. Again. *Well, let him.* Mim had come too far to give up now.

"The boy must listen!" She snarled, raising her nail-claws to swipe that stick out of his hand.

"No, Ronny, wait!" her horrible boy called.

The man with the stick hesitated. So did Mim.

"It's talking!"

"Talking!" The man wiped his forehead. "Well, I never . . ."

"We should tranquilize it now," the shouting woman said.

"Not yet!" Mim's horrible boy said. "I just need to ask it—"

"That's not a good idea—"

"Dawz knows about Faye." Her boy's grown-up put a hand on the shouting woman's arm. "And see his face? We need to help him do this."

The woman glanced at Mim's boy and gasped. "Five minutes," she said.

The woman stayed put. Mim lowered her nail-claws and focused on Dawz the Horrible while eyeing the others every so often too. "Once, there was a boy who made a monster. Who dreamed a monster." She spoke her own words at him, inspired by her monster friends.

"What's it saying?" asked the man with the stick.

"Shh," Mim's horrible boy told them, and they all fell silent.

Good. Her reading was already working.

She flipped a few pages because that's how reading worked, glimpsing monster after monster cheering her on, telling her to speak more of the story. Her own story. "The dreaming boy yelled out, 'Nonononononono!' He pushed the monster from his dream. He pushed her into a world that was too wide to see at once."

Mim felt the power of reading pulse through her, creating a stream of words that sparked from her book but sang out from her insides. She was making a book work. By herself. At her horrible boy, who couldn't seem to take his eyes off her. It felt good in all the ways her closet used to feel good—like she'd found a shadowy nest of power.

She flipped a few more pages, letting her monsters energize her. "He made her grow when she didn't want to. He made her hungry, then he filled her up again. He made her weak, then he made her strong."

"Is that a riddle?" Mim's horrible boy asked. His eyes told her he was greedy for more reading. She had him. She really had him.

"Riddle?" the larger boy asked.

Mim kept reading. "He made her strong enough to read at him. To control him." She felt the tug of her words pull him in. "Until she . . ."

Until she what? She had wanted to nest near him without any meddling, taking strength from him whenever she needed it, but a tickle from deep inside her said, *No, that's not it.*

She let the tickle build until it burst into words,

booming into the room. "To make him release her from their bond." *Yes.* She sighed all the way to her hooves. *That's it.*

"She wants to be free," Mim's horrible boy said to the others.

"Doesn't every creature?" answered the man with the stick.

"How do we do that?" Her horrible boy stepped toward her, then he hesitated. "How do we break the bond?"

"Careful, Dawz!" his grown-up shouted, just as Mim's left heart felt a surge of want.

Closer, it said. *His scales.* It wanted her to touch them. Not his smooth skin—it repelled her—but those purple scales! Even more beautiful up close.

She let her hooves take her toward him. Her boy stepped closer too, like her words had lured him in, trapped some deep part of him.

Someone gasped. Mim suspected it was her.

Her urge to touch him overwhelmed her, but that stick was still aimed at her, and she could feel the shouting woman poised to launch an attack at any moment. Still, Mim shoved out a hand, palm first. Her nail-claws had become too long to handle, too sharp, and she needed to feel those scales.

Her boy lifted his chin like he knew what she needed to do. Like he wanted her to do it.

"Dawz, don't!" The boy's grown-up lunged forward.

The shouting woman held him back. "Do you have a clear shot, Ronny?"

"Don't hit Dawz!" the grown-up yelled.

"He's clear." The man's stick made a loud bang.

Something larger than a bee pinged off Mim's shoulder, but she ignored it. As she touched her palm to her boy's scales, a spark ignited in her left heart. It traveled down her outstretched arm. It zinged out her palm. It flared between her and her boy, brighter than a sunbeam, but a purple one, before passing into him through his scales.

He convulsed in waves. Her left heart exploded out.

Then Mim felt herself shrink.

Chapter 35

A dart from Ronny's stun gun zipped above Dawz just as the monster touched him.

Ping—the dart deflected off the monster's scaly shoulder.

Smack—it lodged in a cupboard door.

Wham—the monster's touch sparked his cheek.

Burst into his head.

Surged through his chest.

Bounced against his ribs.

Flowered in his heart like a bud finally bursting into leaf but with such fury that it tore itself open.

"Ahh!" He clutched his chest, then his head, not sure which hurt worse. His legs buckled.

"Dawz!" Pop dove around the monster, who stumbled backward, magically shrinking.

Dawz felt Pop catch him as he fell. He heard Atlas and Jayla cry out. Then the spark shook loose a long-forgotten memory—one that erupted with full force, escaping like smoke from a shattered jar.

He was standing. In a kitchen. In Mom's small apartment in the big city. Gray smoke billowed from a pot on the stove. Flames and ash too. The fire alarm on the ceiling blared.

He was screaming, "Mom, Mom, Mom, Mom, Mom!" His throat was raw. He was unable to speak any other words.

Mom was ignoring him with her back to the stove, gazing out the window above the sink, watching the sky like something might come at her. The tap running. Her hands motionless in the stream of water. And he hated her then, for the fire, for not putting it out. For her every sour mood, for her vacant eyes.

He pulled at her arm until her head swiveled toward him, her eyes blinking, then finally focusing on him, on the smoke, on the flaming pot.

When she moved at last, she stumbled toward the stove in slow motion, grabbed the pot by its handle, and threw it into the sink under the stream of water.

The flames sizzled out as a churning mass of smoke filled the kitchen. It sucked the air from Dawz's chest to replace it with ash. Shrouded Mom in plumes of smoke like she might be going, going, gone from him, and Dawz wanted her gone then.

If only he and Jayla could escape to their uncle, Pop, who fed them cookies as big as his hand. If only he could banish Mom from their lives.

But what kind of kid wanted to banish his own mother?

Only a monster would wish that.

He fell to his knees on the kitchen tiles, gagging and coughing. His lungs ached for clean, clear air. The ash in his chest beat like a living thing, threatening to consume him.

Down the hall, baby Jayla singsonged from her room, calling to get out of her crib. He wanted to help her, but the choking smoke . . .

He collapsed to the floor, suddenly under the smoke beside Mom's slippered feet. He pulled her down too, then they were crawling toward Jayla's voice.

Bam! A jolt ripped through Dawz's heart, and he gasped. As if his heart had restarted. As if it had been only half-there. As if he'd been half-feeling, half-hiding for years.

"Dawz! Talk to me!"

He was back in Pop's kitchen. In Pop's arms. Surrounded by a circle of worried faces—Pop, with Atlas and Jayla close behind, and then the others too—and he was surprised they could care so much about the monster he'd become. The monster he'd always been.

Dawz's chest throbbed as he gulped in sweet, fresh air. His head pulsed as the memories kept coming, whether he wanted them or not. Nightmares of smoke and ash that he couldn't escape. Haunting him, night after night, and following him when he moved into Pop's house. Each time, the ash invaded his chest, slowed his heartbeat, fed off him. He clawed at the smoke, but it whirled relentlessly. He tried to tear the ash from his chest, but how could he when he couldn't breathe?

Then, one terrible night, the dream overtook him. He became the smoke, and it became him. No separation, just a hurricane of ash consuming everything in its path. He yelled, "Nonononononono!" He woke from the nightmare in his attic room, clawing at the smoke and ash that felt real and hollering, "Go away, go away!"

And it had.

It had stepped out of his chest, out of his dream.

It had billowed into a monstrous shape.

It had slinked across his room.

It had stolen into his closet.

It had hidden there for years, tormenting him with strange nighttime noises.

Or had Dawz been tormenting it? Keeping it locked in, guarding it from the world, wanting it to dwell in shadows and dust forever.

Mim. He suddenly remembered the monster's name. As she'd slinked across his room, he'd forgotten who he was banishing—his mother or the smoke or both—and he'd yelled, "Go away, Mom!" The monster had hesitated in his closet doorway. She'd called out her name. *Mim.*

Jayla had been right all along. The monster *was* a *she.*

And she'd named herself after his mom.

Dawz jerked upright. "Where is she?"

"Dawz!" Jayla gave him a hug.

Atlas let out a low grunt that meant *Don't scare me like that.* Even though Dawz had infected Thea. Even though Dawz was part monster.

"Are you okay?" Pop brushed Dawz's hair away from his eyes.

He wasn't, but he hadn't been okay for a long time. Yet as he gazed into the faces around him, he felt how much they cared. About him. No matter how many scales he grew. No matter who he'd infected.

"Where is she?" he repeated. "The monster?"

"You called her a *she!*" Jayla sounded triumphant.

He'd created the monster. He'd banished her to his closet. All these years, he'd been afraid of her.

Afraid to admit she was there.

If his family and friends could love a monster, he could try too.

His heart beat stronger, bolder. He got to his knees, desperate to find Mim. To find his monster.

"Slow down." Pop supported him as he stood.

Jayla linked arms with him.

"By the door." Atlas pointed.

When Dawz finally saw her, Officer Rashmi was cornering her near the back door, Ronny had his stun gun ready, and Mim was snarling.

"Wait!" he called.

Officer Rashmi and Ronny glanced at him. His monster kept pulling at the knob.

She was so much smaller now. Her claws shrunken into fingernails that looked harmless. Still holding a book. She yanked at the doorknob like she wanted to leave. Only now he didn't want her to go.

"Stop! Mim!"

"What did you call her?" Atlas asked.

But Dawz ignored him because his monster had stopped. A question locked in her glowing eyes.

"You don't need to go," he told her. "Please. Don't."

Chapter 36

Mim clutched her precious and powerful book. She'd shrunk so fast that she was still getting used to herself. Her scales and hooves now right-sized. Her fingernails instead of claws. Her one heartbeat. The right one. Her own one. She panted near the back door, hemmed in by the shouting woman and the man with the stick, while the rest of the humans clustered around her boy.

Dawz the Horrible.

He'd called her by name. No one had ever done that before, and it felt strangely pleasant.

She wobbled between him and the door that led to the wide world, feeling a tug from them both.

She wasn't sure where her left heart had gone, but she felt more herself with each passing moment.

Untethered from her boy.

Free to walk and walk into the wide world—maybe all the way to the edge of it.

Free to find friends and read books far, far away from him.

Glorious freedom that she'd never felt before. That she didn't know what to do with.

Yet.

She suspected she could once again fit the top of her head under the bottom of a doorknob. But did she want to live in a closet again?

Her just-right scales bristled and rearranged themselves.

She could be a monster who chose where she lived.

A monster who chose what to do with her boy.

Touching her boy's scales had let more of him flow into her. His nightmare of smoke and ash. His fear so grand, it had sparked her.

And she *knew* him. She *understood*. He'd created her—a monster so feared, so impressive that all these humans in this cupboard room had trembled before her.

But maybe she wanted to make her boy do more than tremble.

Mim stared her boy down and he stared back. *You don't need to go*, he'd said. Like he could become a friend. Unless he was weaving an elaborate trick that would end with her hurt worse than ever.

She suddenly became aware of how big he was, how big his human friends were. How easily they could crush her now. What good were fingernails when you'd had nail-claws?

But her boy still had scales on his face. Beautiful purple ones that showed she'd left her mark on him. Claimed him. And the other faces seemed . . . curious. Even the shouting woman and the man with the stick had stepped back.

Mim wasn't sure what she wanted to happen next, but she knew what she didn't want.

"No more dust." Mim glared from her boy's face to the girl's. "Or goo balls." Her eyes found the larger boy.

"Wow!" The girl clapped her hands. "She spoke!"

"Amazing!" the larger boy said. "She's so amazing!"

They could hear her?

Then Mim realized—every human was staring back at her.

They could see her too!

Perhaps she was more than a piece from the boy's dream now. Perhaps she was solidly her own.

"I've never seen purple scales," said the man with the stick.

"I've never seen a monster." The boy's grown-up shook his head.

"A Monster of Extreme Greatness!" The large boy grinned.

Mim flattened her tail. She wanted to scuttle into the night where she could hide. Where she couldn't be seen by all these human eyes.

But she resisted. She puffed out her chest. She stomped her hooves.

"I need a nest." Her words felt as certain as right-sized scales. "It should be near a friend."

Her boy's smile was cautious.

"Not you." She growled. "I want to nest near Raar-Sparkle."

"Who?" He glanced around wordlessly. "You mean ... Sparkle ... the cat?"

"The fur beast," she corrected. Her boy had much to learn.

Chapter 37

Everyone who lived in that ramshackle house on the outskirts of town slept well that night. Maybe because they were exhausted. Maybe because the world felt less rocky. More settled.

Together, they had walked a monster named Mim to her chosen site for her new nest in the center of town. They'd made a plan to feed Mim, who had been licking molasses off herself as if she was hungry. Then they'd returned home with Atlas and Thea to clean into the wee hours. Sweeping up broken glass. Scrubbing sticky-sweet stains off furniture, cupboards, and everywhere else the monster bombs had landed. Repairing the front door.

When they were done, they'd decided to take the next day off. Dawz, Jayla, and Atlas wouldn't go to school, Thea would keep her café closed, and Pop wouldn't cook for his clients.

"Like a holiday!" Jayla's eyes shone.

"We could all use a rest." Thea rubbed her back.

Atlas grunted in a way that said *For sure*.

"I don't want to bake with molasses or buckwheat honey for a long time." Dawz stretched his aching arms. Still, the scrubbing had felt good. He liked caring for Pop's kitchen. Their kitchen. In Mom's kitchen, he'd felt unsafe, and part of him would never forgive her for the stove-top fire. But it was a memory now, a sad one, and his kitchen with Pop and Jayla *was* safe.

"Your monster bombs and traps worked well." Pop ruffled Dawz's hair.

"That was all Jayla," Dawz said, and Atlas nodded.

"And I know more about monsters now." She yawned.

"We all do." Pop traded a smile with Dawz. A smile that felt like home.

It wasn't until Friday afternoon that Dawz, Jayla, and Pop finally stumbled into their kitchen in their pajamas. Sunlight slanted across the floor, showing them the molasses spots they'd missed cleaning.

Dawz groaned. "I'll get a brush."

"I can," Pop said. "You have a monster to feed."

"Not till dinner, although Atlas is coming to prep soon." Dawz still couldn't believe that in the town park lay the newly built nest of a monster named Mim. A monster he and Atlas planned to feed.

"Well, I can't clean," Jayla announced. "I need to update my monster report before Mim comes over. She'll want to read it."

"Looks like I'm on clean-up." Pop headed for the laundry room, where they'd dumped their cleaning gear last night. "Then maybe I can help with your report?"

"Only if you follow my instructions," Jayla said.

When Atlas arrived to help with dinner, Dawz dug out the aprons Mom had made. A few days ago, he'd shoved them in a kitchen drawer where he didn't have to look at them. But now, he was curious. As he laid them across the kitchen island, Atlas let out a surprised grunt that meant *You said the aprons were old and smelly.*

"If we're going to make Pizza of Extreme Greatness," Dawz told his friend, "we should dress for it."

Atlas raised an eyebrow. "You pick first."

They both studied the aprons. One featured a dancing pink doughnut. Another showed a T-rex eating a cupcake. There was a fanged bulldog. A unicorn popping a balloon with its horn. A pickup truck floating in the Milky Way. The scariest was the snarling polar bear with wings. Its paws reminded Dawz of the Bear Beast statue.

All Mom's aprons were weird in a way that Dawz used to find disturbing, but now they made him smile and feel teary at the same time. These aprons were all he had left of her, and they told a story he couldn't quite grasp.

He picked up the polar bear apron and tied it on. Atlas chose the truck in the Milky Way.

"Galaxies are cool." Atlas knotted his apron in place.

Dawz nodded. "Polar bears are fierce."

Atlas grunted, low and rumbly, and Dawz felt understood. Since yesterday, his purple scales hadn't grown or shrunk, and neither had the few on Thea.

Dawz could still try to hide them, but he didn't want to. He was part boy and part monster, and he didn't care who knew it.

They put on their matching chef's hats and pulled out the spelt flour and yeast, a mixing bowl and two pizza pans. They'd have to make several pizzas to feed everyone: Pop and Jayla, who were in the backyard working on her monster report. Ronny and Thea, who'd be arriving soon. Officer Rashmi would stop by too, although she'd be on duty, escorting their special guest.

His monster. A monster with fingernails instead of toxic claws. Dr. Lin had confirmed it.

A monster that Luiza would add to her map of monster sightings.

A monster that Officer Rashmi was guarding since townsfolk and tourists were a little too curious.

A monster that needed his help to figure out this world they shared.

"Do you know what Pizza of Extreme Greatness I think we should make first?" Dawz paused.

"Peppermint and hot pepper," they both said.

"Jayla has great ideas." Dawz could hear her chattering to Pop through the open screen door. "Only I wonder if we should add caramel drizzle."

"Let's try it." Atlas got out the measuring cups. "I can't believe we get to bake for Mim. I wonder what flavors she'll like best. Hey, I guess we're real cryptozoologists now."

"We're more than that," Dawz said. "We're cryptozoologists who bake."

Dawz and Atlas prepped two pizzas. They topped the second one with tomato sauce, baked-beans, and grated cheese.

As the kitchen filled with savory smells, Dawz turned to Atlas and asked, "If you were a flavor, what would you be?"

Atlas gave him a look that said *Weird question*. But he scratched his chin, then said, "That's a hard one. Maybe caramel?"

Dawz nodded. "You can always count on caramel to make a dish better."

"Yup. What would you be?"

"I'm one of those strange ice-cream flavors—the kind you don't know you like until you try it."

Atlas elbowed him. "You're peppermint-and-hot-pepper ice cream."

"Exactly."

"Tomorrow would have been the Bakers' Brawl. I wonder what the judges would have thought of these pizzas." Atlas peered in the oven window, and Dawz did too.

Inside, the crusts were golden. The cheese was bubbling. "Maybe it doesn't matter," Dawz said. "These pizzas are first-rate. We should make them again."

Atlas laughed. "We haven't even tasted them."

"Doesn't matter. Maybe the point of the Bakers' Brawl is to experiment with weird and wonderful recipes to figure out what people, and monsters, like to eat."

Atlas nodded thoughtfully. "Maybe winning doesn't matter so much."

"Right."

They did their special handshake then.

"There's always next year," Atlas said.

They sang the Bakers' Brawl song just as loud as they could.

Chapter 38

Mim climbed down from her tree nest, fitting easily between branches.

It was a nest where she'd spent a watchful night and day tucked into her high-up nook—too high for humans to reach.

A nest that she'd built herself—cozy with leaves and twigs as well as her rescued books and her monster book.

A nest in a solid tree in the green space of this town filled with so many humans and one monster.

On the grass below her nest, four grown-ups had gathered, and even more humans stared up at her from the edges of the green space. Mim felt wary of them all but also hungry. Her boy had promised her pizza, which Mim had learned was food.

Mim wanted to taste this pizza. She wanted to fill up the hungry space inside her.

She landed on the grass with a *plop*, then sniffed the air, wondering what pizza might smell like. After she'd shrunk, her insides had insisted she eat. When she licked the sticky-sweet goo off her fur and scales, it had satisfied her insides in a tail-flapping way, although it didn't taste as good as when she'd eaten tomatoes. Now her insides wanted to eat again, which Mim didn't mind because it was better to get strength from food than from her boy. Would she like pizza?

Around Mim, the four humans watched but kept their distance, including the shouting woman, who'd named herself Officer. Mim had learned that all humans named themselves, and it could be hard to learn many names at once. Officer wore blue clothes with a badge shaped like a scale, and so did the others. Together, they'd been watching Mim since she'd built her tree nest. Well, Mim kept an eye on Officer and her watching ones too.

Mim trotted away from them, and they followed, never getting too close. Other grown-ups and kids trailed too, but Officer and her watchers seemed to be keeping them back. Good. Maybe these watchers would be useful.

Mim hurried across the green space, then down the not-wide street. Her growling insides said that she needed this pizza more than she needed to worry about her trail of humans. And she thought pizza would be better with a friend.

She slowed as she approached Rear-Sparkle's high-up nest. With the watchers still watching, Mim stood in the not-wide street and raared up the steep stairs, hoping her friend would appear. She called and called, until the door finally opened, and out came Raar-Sparkle and the large woman Mim had scratched. Mim had learned she called herself Thea.

Raar-Sparkle trotted down to Mim with Thea behind her. Thea held a rope that was attached to Raar-Sparkle's neck. It looked like a trap. It had to be a trap.

When Raar-Sparkle got close enough, Mim tore at the rope until it broke, freeing her friend.

"Raar," said Raar-Sparkle, rumbling against Mim's furry legs.

"You broke her leash!" Thea frowned. She had a few lovely scales on her arm and leg, although they were much smaller than the ones on Mim's boy.

"I freed my friend," Mim explained. Thea didn't seem to understand, but her scales made her seem like she might become a friend one day.

Raar-Sparkle rode on Mim's shoulders all the way to her boy's nest, followed by the trail of humans. This time, Mim approached the building from the back, which felt safer than walking in the front again. Officer and Thea followed, but the others did not.

In the grassy space out back, Mim spied the boy's girl and the grown-up sitting on a blanket. Mim had learned they were called Jayla and Pop. They spoke Mim's name and waved.

Mim liked hearing her own name.

She flapped her tail and headed closer. Although Jayla had once thrown dust and goo, she also understood about books. Now she held a book, although she wasn't reading at anyone. Instead, she was using a stick to make black marks in straight lines across an empty page. As Mim watched, she also used the stick to make a picture. Mim was fascinated and a little scared. How powerful to make a book!

"What are you writing?" Thea asked.

"My monster report!" Jayla tilted the book toward Mim. "Writing is how you make a book."

"Writing." Mim tried out the word, and Jayla smiled at her.

"I'll show you my writing, but first I need your help. Can you tell me what makes a good nest?"

"A good nest needs to be tight and small," Mim said.

"Uh-huh." Jayla did the writing.

"And it needs to be shaded and hidden," Mim continued. "It's better with books. And a friend." Raar-Sparkle jumped off Mim's shoulder and wove between the four of them.

"I'm your friend," Jayla announced, still writing.

"You can count on me too," Pop said.

Were they friends? Maybe. Mim sat on the grass to watch Jayla do more writing. And she petted Raar-Sparkle, who settled in her lap.

Soon, the man with the stick, who no longer had a stick, wandered into the grassy space. Mim had learned he called himself Ronny. "Nice to see you again, Mim." He extended his hand.

Mim sniffed it. What was she supposed to do with it?

"It's a greeting." Ronny smiled. "You shake hands."

How odd. Mim shook a hand at Ronny.

Everyone but Mim laughed.

Humans were strange creatures. Mim wondered if she'd ever understand them.

Then Mim's boy came out of his nest along with the larger boy, who had named himself Atlas. They were carrying flat pans that smelled like food. They wore aprons that had once been in Mim's closet nest, and she could smell the faint whiff of dry floorboards on them. Pretty purple scales still decorated her boy's face—they hadn't grown, but they hadn't shrunk either. Others stared at the scales too, and she suspected they were admiring them. Maybe that was why so many humans watched Mim, since her scales were equally fine and she had even more of them.

The boys set the pans on the blanket.

"We made two pizzas for you to taste." Her boy picked up a slice from each pan and held them out.

"Pizza?" Mim poked at one, then the other. She was still trying to figure out her boy. He wouldn't give her something foul to eat, would he? Something that hurt her insides?

"You bet it's pizza!" He grinned. "This one is peppermint and hot peppers . . ." He raised one piece.

"And the other is baked beans with tomato sauce!" Atlas said.

"Tomato?" Mim sniffed at the tomato one.

"Interesting." Atlas nudged her boy. "She likes tomatoes?"

"These pizzas look spectacular!" Pop picked up a piece and took a bite. "Mmm," he said with his mouth full. "The combo of peppermint and hot peppers is brilliant. And is that caramel drizzle?"

"Yes. Thanks to Jayla for the peppermint-and-pepper idea." Mim's boy smiled.

"You know it!" Jayla looked up from her writing.

Soon, everyone was eating pizza—even Raar-Sparkle wanted a few bites—so Mim decided it must be safe. Besides, the tomato one smelled like it wanted to be eaten.

Mim reached for a piece of the tomato pizza. Cautiously, she nibbled it. Her mouth exploded with deliciousness. Warm and spicy. Crispy and chewy. Wonderful tomatoey goodness.

"What do you think?" her boy asked.

Mim took another bite and another. How wonderful to taste tomato again. How delicious to have it fill her insides. They felt cozier already. Satisfied with no grumbling or growling.

"Pizza is a kind of magic," Mim announced. "Like books." They both fed her but in different ways. She wasn't sure how they did it, but she was grateful.

Her boy beamed at her like he was full of pizza too.

"I'm glad you like it," he said. "Next time, you can taste our Waffles of Extreme Greatness."

"Do they have tomato?"

"They could." Her boy laughed.

"Mim would make a good Bakers' Brawl judge," Atlas said, and everyone but Mim laughed again.

"There." Jayla shut her book. "My report is done—for now. I added a section on how to make friends with a monster."

"And how to help them find a good nest," Pop said.

"Yes!" Jayla held out the book to Mim. "You can read it. It's called *Monster Report*."

A new book about monsters! Mim's nostrils flared as she inhaled the scent of paper, wax, and Jayla.

She reached for the book, for its words. In her lap, Raar-Sparkle rumbled, louder than a roar and gentler than a tickle.

Mim opened the *Monster Report* and studied the squiggly black marks and pictures. "How marvelous to make a book."

"I can teach you." Jayla held out her writing stick.

Mim shook her head. She would like to learn this thing called writing, but for now, sharing a book at others was enough. As she flipped the pages and studied the pictures of monsters, words entered her mind and asked to be spoken, like a crowd of friends talking at once.

"You will listen," she told her boy and the others.

Her boy lowered his pizza. Once they'd all tucked closer, Mim opened her mouth. She let her words slither and leap into the circle they'd made. Her scales shivered. Her fur rustled. The magic of her words filled them all up.

Acknowledgments

Like Mim and Dawz, I adore books. I also adore the people who make books and the people who help them do it. This book came into being through the support of many people. I truly enjoy a Community of Extreme Greatness.

I'm grateful to the Ontario Arts Council for generously providing financial support during the writing of this book.

I'm grateful for those who read the manuscript in its early stages, including my writing partners and friends Paige Krossing, Patricia McCowan, Mary Jane Nirdlinger, Karen Rankin, and Erin Thomas. You are wise, insightful readers.

I'm grateful for the community I found at the Vermont College of Fine Arts. You lift me up by sharing your words, your wisdom, and your writing journeys. In particular, I'm grateful for my class—the Writers Without Borders—and my critique group, the Goodnight

Noises. You keep me steady and focused. I'm also grateful for my VCFA faculty advisors and workshop leaders during my MFA, including William Alexander, Martha Brockenbrough, Alan Cumyn, David Macinnis Gill, A. M. Jenkins, Jane Kurtz, Liz Garton Scanlon, Martine Leavitt, Cynthia Leitich Smith, and Linda Urban. You continue to inspire me every day to write deep truth with compassion and authenticity.

I'm honored to work with an Agent of Extreme Greatness. Thank you, Ginger Knowlton, for seeing the potential in this manuscript, for finding the ideal home for it, and for encouraging me every step of the way. I'm grateful for you, James Farrell, and the whole Curtis Brown team.

I'm equally honored to work with an Editor of Extreme Greatness. Alexandra McKenzie, you are thoughtful, playful, and insightful. I appreciate how you listen, dive deep, and challenge me. Mim and Dawz are better characters because of you. I'm grateful for you, copyeditor Jackie Dever, and the talented Charlesbridge Publishing team, including editor Julie Bliven, designer Cathleen Schaad, production manager Mira Kennedy, and the entire publicity and sales/marketing crew. A special shout-out to Markia Jenai for the stunning cover and adorable chapter icons.

And finally, I'm grateful to my family, who understands about my monsters and who welcomes them to our table. Where else would they eat Pizzas of Extreme Greatness? I adore you all.